ABBADON

BECA LEWIS

Published by:
Perception Publishing
https://perceptionpublishing.com

This book is a work of fiction. All characters in this book are fictional. However, as a writer, I have, of course, made some of the book's characters composites of people I have met or known.

Table of Contents

One

I slumped further into my chair, all my hopes slowly dissolving, soon to disappear. A few days ago, my expectations had been high. We were going to be proactive. We were going after Abbadon before he came after us. After stopping Abbadon's last attempt at mass destruction, our entire team had taken time to visit family and friends and put our affairs in order.

All of us said goodbye to those that loved us and promised them that we would see them again. But no one was fooled. It was just as likely that most of us would never return. My father's housekeeper, Berta, hugged me and told me everything would be okay. What else was she was supposed to say?

One by one we had returned to the Castle, rested and hopeful. We had been cheered by the signs of improvement all over the Kingdom. However, my father, the King of Zerenity, had not come back to the Castle with me.

When one of Abbadon's monsters killed my mother, my father had returned to our hometown of Eiddwen, laid down on his bed, and hadn't gotten up again until just a few weeks ago. And although he decided to live after we rescued him and all the villagers in Eiddwen, my father had not yet decided to return to being the King. I was hoping that once we defeated Abbadon, he would change his mind.

Although the title of Princess Kara Beth, future Queen of Zerenity, sounds good in fairy tales, in real life it is not a job that I wanted. Actually, I didn't want any of this. But the choice was between letting my father's evil brother, Abbadon, destroy the Kingdom, or stepping up and fighting.

We had all made that choice. To fight. Really, what other choice could we have made? But we needed a plan, and so far every idea we had come up with appeared impossible.

I glanced around the table at the people I had come to love and admire. They all looked as dejected as I felt. Everyone was there, except for Earl and Ariel. I assumed they were off somewhere bringing water and wind where it was needed. Whatever our plan turned out to be, I knew they would be there to support it.

It was hard to believe that less than a year ago I had been living what I thought of now as a normal life. Then with the help of Suzanne, a liaison between Earth and Erda, I had stepped through the portal between the two dimensions. I had left Earth as a pre-teen and returned to Erda as a young woman.

Let me tell you, that was a shock of a lifetime. But it was only the beginning of the shocks waiting for me. However, at that moment, looking down at a fully-developed body, it felt as if I was going insane. Then to make it worse, Suzanne had disappeared, and two beings that I had never seen before greeted me. One looked like a flower turned into a person and the other like a block of wood that walked. Beru and Ruta. Now I can't imagine life without them.

I got over the age change pretty quickly. There were so many other things going on that it faded into the background. Besides, age is almost meaningless in Erda. Time is counted on a completely different scale than it is in the Earth Realm. And in Erda, everyone gets to choose when to stop aging. Or at least slow it down until it is barely noticeable. That was one thing I hadn't decided to do yet. To slow down my aging. Or maybe I did before, but I don't remember it now. Just add that to the list of things I still don't remember.

What I do remember is my two short lifetimes in the Earth Realm as Hannah. I loved my time there. I had thought I was a human child. But once I stepped through that portal, I found out the truth. My Erda parents had sent me to Earth as a protective measure. Abbadon had started to threaten the Kingdom of Zerenity, and they thought it was better to send me away. Then things got worse, and my father and mother were no longer the ones making decisions, so the people I now call my team brought me back.

There was a problem, though. I couldn't remember anything when I returned. And I had very little time to recall the magical skills I had once had before my first encounter with Abbadon's monsters. Even now, so many things are still dark empty holes in my memory and no one has decided to fill them in for me yet.

Before we left to visit our families, Professor Link had promised us something new that would help with our plans, but so far he had made no mention of it.

Instead, the whole attack-Abbadon-first idea seemed over before we even began. At least that was how it felt to me. We had been at this for days and days, and a solution seemed further and further away. When we were on the defense, we were more successful. With a combination of skill, luck, and perhaps providence being on our side, we had managed to stop Abbadon's monsters—the Shrieks, Shatterskin, and Deadsweep.

But we knew we would not be able to stop another Abbadon attack. Instead, we had decided that it was time for us to go after him first. At the time it had sounded possible, but now it appeared that it wasn't going to be.

To begin with, we knew it would be the height of foolishness to think that he didn't know we would be coming after him. And what he might have in store for us as we came his way boggled the mind. My father's brother was brilliant.

But that wasn't the end of the problem. How could we get to Abbadon without being seen? Abbadon had destroyed the entire western part of the kingdom. Shatterskin lived up to its name; everything that had been growing was dead, uprooted and barren. We would be moving across an empty plain with no place to hide.

Every tree, every building had been destroyed. It was a suicide mission which would accomplish nothing, which is why I have been waiting for someone to tell me a better plan.

Instead, we have talked over everything until I want to scream. Even the Priscillas, the three fairies who were usually full of cheer, were somber. They hadn't even bothered to come to the meeting this morning. I couldn't blame them.

Two

"That's what he looks like? Are you kidding?"

In my hand, I held a picture drawn by a sketch artist of a man that Zeid claimed was Abbadon. If this was him, then Abbadon, the man who had been terrorizing everyone, had been living in the Kingdom of Zerenity for years. Right under our noses. Not back in a Castle in the middle of desolation. No, right in our home.

This normal looking man was the one that wanted to destroy all life? The one we had spent the last year fighting the monsters he had created?

"What did you think he would look like?" Zeid asked.

"Not like my father, that's for sure. I guess I was envisioning a huge scary beast. Or maybe horns would be growing out of his head, or blood would be dripping off of huge teeth."

I shook my head. It was stupid of me to be thinking of him that way. After all, we had learned that Abbadon had been hiding in plain sight inside the Castle. He had passed himself off as one of the caretakers, while he learned everything he needed to know about us.

It would have been easier if Abbadon did look like a monster. Perhaps then I would be able to accept that he was stronger and wiser than us. But this was a man who could blend in anywhere. He had allowed himself to age to what looked like maybe fifty Earth years. My father Darius had done the same thing.

They both had short steel-gray hair, and if the picture was accurate, Abbadon was about the same height as my father. This man had a slight stubble of a beard, and it looked good on him. His eyes didn't give away the evil mind that lived inside of him. Instead, they were soft and somewhat sad brown eyes.

"Are you sure this is him?" I asked again.

"Yes. Villagers have identified him as the man selling the walking sticks, and the people in the Castle who saw him say he was the same man."

Zeid and I were sitting at one of the smaller tables in the Castle's atrium. The meeting had broken up with no solutions in sight. Everyone needed a break. Now I suspected the break was to give Zeid time to show me the picture.

I thought that he had chosen this place to show me because he knew I loved this garden. No matter how gloomy the world seemed, the flowers and trees that grew in the atrium always made me feel better.

That was Zeid. Always thinking of me first, and not for the first time I wondered how I could be so lucky to have him as my betrothed. The first time I had seen him in Erda, I didn't remember him, but my heart did. I still didn't know if our future marriage had been arranged, or if we chose it, but it didn't matter anymore. I had told him I loved him.

I looked across the table at Zeid's azure eyes and dark hair that framed one of those handsome faces that almost don't look real, and smiled at him.

Zeid was my best friend, my sparring partner, and the man who put up with all my confusion after returning to Erda and not remembering anything about my life before Earth.

"Has everyone seen this picture?"

"Yes."

"Why am I always last? Shouldn't I be first? I mean you want me to become who I am here in Erda, Princess Kara Beth, and yet you, and the rest of the team, show me things last. Why is that?"

"That's something you need to take up with Professor Link and Niko. You know they make those kinds of decisions. If it helps you feel any better, I just saw this picture today too, and then they asked me to show it to you during the break."

"Why?"

When Zeid didn't answer me, I asked again, "Why? Why not show it to me during the meeting? What did they think I was going to do? Start screaming, yelling, jumping up and down? Why?"

Before Zeid could answer, he was saved by one of my favorite sounds. A Sound Bubble's harmony was coming closer. I glanced up and saw the atrium roof open, and the bubble slowly descended. Inside the bubble were two people we had met in our last battle with Abbadon.

"Why are Garth and Anne here?"

Zeid shrugged again. He either was pretending not to know what was going on, or he really didn't.

Garth and Anne were twins and well known for the ability to travel between dimensions. After Abbadon froze the entire town of Kinver in a portal that was locked in time and space, the twins assisted Suzanne with the town's release.

For the first time in days, I felt a glimmer of hope. Maybe Professor Link did have a plan after all.

Three

Before I got a chance to welcome Garth and Anne, Professor Link arrived and whisked them away. What the ziffer was going on? Why couldn't I talk to them?

I was about ready to jump up and run after them even though it was evident that I wasn't supposed to when the Priscillas came zooming around the corner and landed on my head. All three. Which perhaps says as much about how big of a head I have as to how important it was that I didn't follow Link.

"Okay, I'm not going," I said, as I tried to pull Pris out of my hair. Her sisters, La and Cil, had already arranged themselves on my shoulders, but Pris loves to pull my hair to get my attention. Or just because she can.

She has always been like that. The three sisters have been my companions since my childhood. When we were younger, we loved getting into trouble together. Now our focus is more on stopping trouble, but that didn't change their personalities.

The three sisters are easy to tell apart. Not only do they behave differently, but they also have some distinctive physical attributes. You would think the Pris, as the older sister, wouldn't be the one who wore pigtails. But she does. Probably, knowing Pris, it was an act of defiance.

Pris can be moody, but she is fierce about protecting what, and who, she loves. Pris has a multitude of faces that can stop grown men in their tracks. When the little blue star on her forehead starts to wrinkle, watch out, trouble is brewing.

All three fairies can pull a pout that could last for days, especially if they don't think I trust them. I was learning that they were always right and that I needed to stop trying to control what they do. Fairies do what they want when they want, especially Pris.

Cil is the middle sister. Her green eyes spark when she is angry, or happy. Mostly, Cil is cheerful and easy going. She gets along with everyone. Sometimes she acts as the buffer between Pris and their youngest sister, La. I doubt that Cil likes that role very much, but she is good at it.

I patted Cil on the head, and she slid down into the pocket of my tunic. It is one of her favorite places to sleep. Sometimes she forgets she is in there and falls out as she is waking up. Usually, I catch her in time, but when she drops the whole way, she is never hurt, just embarrassed.

La has a white streak in her hair and is the quietest of the three of them. A little shy, she is sometimes intimidated by Pris. However, when there are essential things to be said, La is often the one that speaks up and makes sure everyone who needs to say something gets a chance. La also has a crush on Zeid, and can often be found on my shoulder staring at him. I don't mind. It means someone other than me is watching out for him.

The picture of Abbadon lay on the table. Pris flew off my head, down to the picture, and stamped on it. I knew exactly how she felt. I wanted to stamp on it too.

"Okay, now that you have kept me from going after Garth and Anne, why not tell me what's going on."

Zeid just shook his head, and the fairies shook their heads

along with him. It was ridiculous, all four shaking their heads at me.

I would have complained more loudly and perhaps gone after Link anyway except I saw Beru and Ruta coming my way. Now, you might not want to piss off a fairy, but for sure, you never want to cross Beru and Ruta.

To look at the two of them, you would never think that they would end up as best friends. But they are. Beru had told me that she considered Ruta a brother. I know there is a story or two that I don't know that caused that to happen, and I am hoping to hear it someday.

I know a little more about Beru than I do about Ruta. I consider Beru's hometown of Kinver my second home. Five men from Kinver had gone with us to fight the Shrieks and Shatterskin. Only four came back, and I felt I owed the village my thanks for their sacrifice. But it isn't just that. James was one of the men who came with us, and I adopted him as a second father, or he adopted me, I'm not sure which came first. But he calls me Hannah, and promised me that Kinver would always welcome me as one of their daughters.

James has a daughter, Liza. It was her gift to me of a little star necklace that I wore around my neck that helped us overcome the odds and defeat Abbadon. It allows me to see the world in 4D instead of the usual 3D version. It's incredible how much is going on around us that we can't see.

I suppose it's to our benefit to not see all that all the time, but it is so beautiful sometimes I wish that I could stay there. I only use the star when it is necessary because I promised Liza to never just play with it. Liza might be a young girl, but she possesses wisdom and skills far beyond her age. She can see 4D at any time she chooses, and she has told me that I too have that ability.

It's true. I have done it once or twice, but it doesn't come easily or often. It's something that I am still working on.

John, James' brother and one of the men from Kinver who helped us fight Abbadon's monsters, is the naysayer in the group. He is always questioning our plans. At first, we thought he might be the mole that was giving away our secrets to Abbadon. We soon found that wasn't true. Besides, we need him to question our decisions. More than once he had helped refine what we were doing. And of course, Abbadon was in the Castle the whole time, finding out our secrets all on his own.

The men from Kinver were going to stay home this time. Assuming we had a plan. Liza told me the last time she saw me that I would know what choice to make when it was time. I wondered what she knows that I don't.

Four

Beru and Ruta drew a chair up to our table, and one of the metal toadstools made his way over to the table. I called all of them George because I wasn't sure which ones were which. But I was reasonably sure that the one at our table was the real George. He already had some goodies on the plate that was on top of his head, along with cups of coffee and water.

When I patted him on the shoulder, he purred. "He only does that for you, you know," Zeid said.

I didn't know that, but I smiled at George and said, "Thank you." George did a little shiver and moved away.

"So what's going on? How come you two are out here?"

"Just keeping you company," Beru replied sweetly. As if that fooled me.

"You're keeping me from going after Anne and Garth. Come on, admit it, that's why you are all here. Why am I kept out of these things?"

Ruta grunted at me. That wasn't unusual. I got a lot of grunts and humphs from Ruta. When he and Beru met me at the portal, it was apparent that he didn't like me, or held a grudge against me, and he was only there to greet me because it was his duty.

Once I discovered that Abbadon had destroyed his whole village, I began to understand his resentment. Perhaps he thought that if I hadn't been someplace else, I might have been able to save them.

Although I would be inclined to take on that guilt, we both knew it wasn't true. My mother had been there visiting his people, and she died too. If anyone could have stopped Shatterskin then, it would have been her. Instead, it took all of us working as a team to stop Shatterskin and his minions the Shrieks.

I used to call Ruta, Mr. Grumpy Head. I hate to think what he might have called me. But over time we have both overcome our initial distrust. Now I would trust Ruta with anything. Not only is he the healer in our group, but he can also do things no one else can do. I've never seen it, but I understand that he travels through the trees—not the way we do as we walk through a forest, or sometimes through the overstory. No, Ruta becomes part of the trees. Somehow Ruta changes his physical presence into a form of energy that moves through the roots, trunks, and branches of trees.

When he is with us, he travels our way. However, on his own, he can move much faster. I know very little about Ruta's background. Was his village the only village with beings like him? He never visits anyone of his own kind, at least as far as I know. On the other hand, traveling by tree, maybe he does. How would I know?

Although Beru had a hometown to return to, her family wasn't there. They had left at the first sign of trouble, and since then no one has heard from them. That means neither Beru or Ruta have a family, perhaps that is one reason they are so happy being together.

I wiggled my fingers at Ruta and winked. This time he

humphed. But he didn't fool me. He loved it.

"I know it looks like we are stopping you, but instead we are simply keeping you company," Beru said, her entire face lighting up with her smile.

"That's what I mean. You're keeping me company while planning is going on, aren't you? Admit it."

Beru is a terrible liar, so I directed my question at her. This time she just smiled back at me.

"You really are just keeping me company?"

"Yep. We are in the dark as much as you are, so we thought, why not spend some quality time together?

"Oh, and Niko said since there are no more meetings today, there will be classes after lunch."

I grimaced. I was right. There was an ulterior motive for the two of them showing up. Classes. I haven't been in classes since returning from Eiddwen. Sometimes I love my classes. Sometimes I don't. But I know they are essential.

Although I have become more skilled at some of the magic I used to know, I have a long way to go. Besides, if we were going to go after Abbadon, I had to be in better physical shape than I am. It is a long trek across the country.

The atrium roof slid back, and we all glanced up to see a beautiful dragon drop down into the garden. Within seconds the dragon morphed into Suzanne. It never got old watching her do that. But Suzanne had told me once that although it looked easy and effortless, it wasn't. There was always a moment of pain during the transition. Now that I know that, I wince every time she shifts. Suzanne never does.

I hadn't known that Suzanne left the Castle. But then, do I expect to know everything about everyone all the time? Yes. I pretty much do. Besides I thought she was with Garth and Anne.

"No, Link took them to Leif and Sarah," Suzanne pushed into my head. "I needed to get outside."

Telepathy was something I had gotten used to using, although I still have to remind myself not to let everyone know what I am thinking. However, for the most part, I have everything shut off except the channel we all kept open to communicate with one another.

I felt that there was another reason Suzanne had gone out with the dragons, but there was no point in asking her now. Sooner or later we would all find out.

"Is everyone coming to lunch?" I asked Suzanne.

Instead of answering, she gestured with her head, looking for a moment almost like a bird, to the other side of the atrium where the other members of our team were slowly filing in. It seemed as if everyone was coming to lunch except for the five meeting in secret.

I slipped the picture of Abbadon into the pocket of my tunic. Since everyone had seen the picture already, there was no reason to flash it around and ruin everyone's appetite. During this past year, I had learned to enjoy every minute we weren't off fighting Abbadon's monsters.

From the look on everyone's face, they agreed. Garth and Anne had come to the Castle for a reason, and once we found out what that was, it was likely we wouldn't have much time for simple pleasures like having lunch together.

Five

During lunch, Aki told me to come to her classroom first. That was probably to give my lunch enough time to settle before heading to the practice yard with Niko. Niko's training sessions were never easy, and sometimes they were downright brutal.

Beru walked me to Aki's studio just as she did the first time when I had no idea what I would find there. That seemed like years ago, even though it had been less than a year since I came through the portal between the two dimensions.

As always, Beru said she'd see me later and let me walk into the studio on my own. Aki wasn't there yet, so I sat down and waited. There was no tea table set in the center of the room, so I figured it wasn't going to be a storytelling day.

Either way, it was okay with me. I enjoyed Aki's lessons. The first time I saw her, Aki was floating into the room a few inches off the floor. Brilliant person that I am, I called her Miss Floaty until I learned her real name. It turned out that she could levitate, and come and go at will. Two amazing skills. One minute she will be there, and the next—poof—gone.

Other members of our team can transport themselves somewhere in the blink of an eye, like Zeid. But I didn't think that was what Aki was doing.

Maybe it was because I never knew her to end up somewhere else. I thought perhaps she didn't go anywhere at all, just became invisible. That was my new theory, and I hoped at some point to be able to test it. But Aki was another one who kept to herself.

Aki had never mentioned family. And if she had friends outside of our team, I didn't know of them. Within the team, I suspect that she and Professor Link are having a thing. I don't know what kind of thing the two of them are having though. Maybe they are just best friends.

However, I suspected it was more than that. I had caught Link watching Aki in a way that seemed much more intense than colleagues. Aki is harder to read, but once I saw them standing in the hallway together, and there were definitely some sparks flying between them.

Perhaps they are waiting for more peaceful times before allowing themselves an open romantic relationship like the one between Zeid and me. Peaceful times will only come when we have stopped Abbadon. That is one thing everyone is clear about. How to stop him was the part that wasn't clear.

Waiting for Aki, I dropped into one of the many stretches that she had taught me. Many of the stretches are yoga stretches, and others are ones I have never seen before. All of them are both painful and pleasurable at the same time. I know that flexibility is a crucial component of strength and endurance. Being flexible means I will not be fighting against my own stiff and unyielding muscles, wasting energy.

I was in the middle of a stretch when I felt the air shift in the room. I looked up, and there was Aki, floating just inches off the floor, appearing out of nowhere.

Taking a chance that Aki would be in the mood for talking, I asked her, "Is that something that all your people can do, or is it a magical skill that belongs only to you?"

"Are you asking if you could learn how to do it?" Aki countered, skillfully leading me away from learning more about her.

I tried it again. "Yes, I would like to learn how. Is it possible? Or is it only people like you who can do it?"

Aki did something she rarely does. She laughed. "Nice try, Kara Beth. But all I am going to say in answer to your question is, yes, perhaps you could learn how to do it. As for my people, that will remain a mystery to you for a bit longer.

"However, I don't want to waste time on that kind of training for now. If it happens, it happens. Right now you can put into your belief system that it's possible. Imagine yourself levitating. Then when the time is right, perhaps the solution to how to do it will present itself to you.

"Today, let's quickly review your flexibility routine, and then I want to go over the story I told you about the two bored brothers on the spaceship."

My pulse quickened. I had hoped to ask Aki a few questions about that story. Maybe this would be the day that it happened.

It turned out that it wasn't. Although I had retained much of the flexibility that Aki had pushed me into, there were a few parts of my body that had reverted to stiffness. That meant extra time stretching.

I hadn't noticed how stiff I had become. Probably from sitting as much as we had been. In one particularly difficult stretch, Aki stood on my back to push me past the point that wouldn't yield.

Once I got over wanting to scream at her to get off, I noticed that the pressure of her standing on my back kept changing. One minute she would be so light, I didn't think she was there, and another she was heavier than I thought Zeid would be if he were standing on me.

I was doing my best to relax through all that, so it didn't dawn on me right away that she was not only helping me stretch, she was also demonstrating something about her ability to levitate. Was she defying gravity? Or was something lifting her off of me? Or did this have something to do with her ability to flash out of being present?

"What if all three of those things went together?" I heard Aki ask me.

Before I left to train with Niko, Aki took both my hands in hers and said, "You are letting your self-importance begin to fade away. This is good. Keep going. Get lighter."

Even before she released my hands, she faded away. As she did, I could feel the touch of her hands lighten, and then she was gone.

Beru was standing in the doorway waiting for me. I hadn't heard her arrive. For the first time, it occurred to me that perhaps she could do what Aki was doing.

Beru, as always, read what I was thinking and said, "Sometimes. Now let's get going. You know how Niko hates being kept waiting. Besides, Zeid is waiting too."

That was enough for me. I reached for Beru's hand, and we giggled our way to Niko's.

I wasn't kidding about enjoying every moment. When I had seen Beru frozen in time and space, I thought I would die. I will be forever grateful to Garth, Anne, and Suzanne for opening a portal to where they were and freeing them.

I wasn't planning to let a moment of good times with Beru slip away from me ever again. If it meant skipping down the hall together, then that was what we were going to do.

Maybe we could beat Abbadon by being happy. Well, probably not. But at least I didn't want to let him take my happiness away.

Six

The training with Niko turned out to be a little less brutal than I was anticipating. As usual, Zeid was with me, which always makes it more enjoyable, even though Zeid never backs down and I never win. After each defeat, either Zeid or Niko laughs at me and reminds me that even though I didn't win, I learned, which is winning. Right.

However, I do have to admit that I appreciate that neither of them treats me as if I am incapable of winning. Someday I will. I'm still clumsy, and I don't think that will ever change. But I can get better, and that's all that Niko asks of us.

Watching Niko demonstrate what he wanted us to do was always mind-blowing. Besides being able to do everything with ease, he is easy to look at too. He is a bronze statue that moves like a gazelle. Yes, that had been my name for him at first—the Gazelle man.

However, there is much more to Niko than his martial arts skill and his looks.

I remember him lying in the tree branches looking like a snake. I had wondered if he was a chameleon or shapeshifter, and I still don't know the answer. There was also the time that the dragons picked us up by the shoulders and lifted us away from the danger we were in from the thought-worm tree. Ruta covered his eyes, and I held my breath. But Niko spread his arms and pretended to be flying. Yes, there is much more to Niko than meets the eye.

After our sparring session, we stayed in the practice yard to do some magic training, which is often harder than the physical exercise. Niko had Zeid make all of us invisible and hold it longer than his previous record. Then he had Zeid teleport both of us back and forth across the yard until he ran out of energy.

Then it was my turn. I had to practice shooting lightning from both my hands. After that, it was my turn to go back and forth across the practice field, but I had to fly.

To finish off my training for the day, I had to practice using my bracelet to stun some poor rabbits that Niko had collected. He said that they volunteered, but I still hated doing it.

However, they weren't hurt and afterward I sat on the ground petting them and giving them the treats that Beru had brought out. After thanking the rabbits for their participation, we opened the small door between the practice field wall and the outside grounds, and they went scampering off as happy as can be.

I suppose they knew the same way that we did that it was vital for me to learn to adjust how much force field to put out without hurting anyone, just enough to stop them.

My bracelet came from my mother who had left it with Professor Link to give to me when I returned to Erda. I am still not sure why she left it for me. Did she know she was going to die at Ruta's village? And if she had it with her, would she have lived? I added those questions to the running list I have that may never have an answer.

Sarah had explained to me how the bracelet worked, and I had used it for the first time to stun the villagers who had been infected with the Deadsweep thought-worms. Thankfully, the worms are dead and gone, and everyone who was infected has been restored to full health. But not before almost the entire population of Dalry, the village near the Castle, died.

Only forty-two people survived, including the wife and daughters of the first man to die in Dalry. We had harbored the survivors within the Castle walls until Deadsweep was over. Then they returned to their homes to bury the dead, mourn the loss of their families and friends, and attempt to recover.

I knew that Mayor Tom would do everything in his power to make it so. However, we all understood that it would leave a scar that would last all our lifetimes. The two little girls had gone from being light and carefree to withdrawn and sullen. I wanted more than anything to return their father to them. It was impossible, of course.

It wasn't just Dalry that was affected by this horrible thing Abbadon had released. There were thousands of people who died throughout the Kingdom of Zerenity. What made it even more tragic is that they died at the hands of friends and family. The thought-worms had bored into the heads of the victims causing their brains to malfunction. I'll never get the pictures out of my head of what people had done to each other.

Once Abbadon discovered that we knew how to stop the thought-worms, remove them, and heal the damaged parts of the brain, he moved on to other forms of death and destruction.

First, he burned down the entire village of Eiddwen, my father's hometown and the town where I grew up when we were not living in the Castle. If Suzanne and Aki had not been there, the entire village would have perished.

That was Abbadon's intention after all. He wanted to kill the King along with everyone else and erase all our memories from the face of the planet. It would have devastated the entire

Kingdom and broken all of our hearts if he had succeeded. I'm sure that's what he wanted.

Instead, Suzanne and Ava managed to open a portal door and usher everyone in the village inside, saving them from the fire. But the entire town was trapped inside the portal for days. Suzanne didn't want to open the back portal door to another dimension and wasn't sure when it would be safe to open the door to the Erda dimension. She and Berta had trusted that eventually we would arrive and let them know it was safe to exit. Berta had left a clue to tell me where they were, and that's how we found them.

Abbadon had done the opposite with Beru's village of Kinver. He left the town alone. Instead, he threw everyone into a portal and then froze them there.

Although I could see them by using the blue star necklace to see 4D, I couldn't do anything to save them. I could see Beru, Liza, and the brothers frozen in what looked like a block of ice. But in reality, Abbadon had frozen them in time and space.

Liza was able to send me a thought picture with the word "portal," and that's how we knew what he had done to them. However, it took the dimension-traveling abilities of Garth, Anne, and Suzanne to step into the portal and release them.

Whatever Abbadon was planning next would be even more frightening. We had to stop him before that happened.

Seven

The session with Niko had lasted well into the afternoon. By the time we had fed the rabbits, Zeid and I were thoroughly wrung out and ready for food for ourselves. We were halfway down the hall to the atrium when I heard the words "Pumpkin Toes," and I started running. I didn't need to see who had yelled those words. There was only one person who called me silly names like Pumpkin Toes.

It was Teddy the Whistle Pig. I knew that Teddy was a Whistle Pig. However, except for the two front teeth that gave him away, he looked more like a big giant teddy bear, unlike the whistle pigs, otherwise known as groundhogs in the Earth dimension. That meant his name, Teddy, suited him perfectly. I figured if Teddy was there, then at least one of the Ginete brothers was with them, and I was right.

Walking beside him was Pita, the oldest of the five brothers. Pita and Teddy looked nothing alike, and yet I knew that Whistle Pigs and Ginete are related.

Someday I would have to find out how. The only thing they have in common is they both live underground, and they are brilliant at figuring out solutions for defeating Abbadon's monsters.

They are also both pacifists, and will not fight in a battle. Instead, as we worked to stop Abbadon's monsters, they supplied everything we needed. It was in their underground homes that we took refuge in when we were under attack, and it was in their laboratories that the solution was found for stopping the thought-worms. We couldn't have won any of the battles against Abbadon's monsters without them.

But where Teddy is big, loud, and effusive, the five Ginete brothers are small and quiet. Most of the time. Their huge golden eyes are always taking in everything going on around them. When I first met them, I thought they were dwarfs, but was told never to call them that. There must be a story in there somewhere.

When I finished hugging Teddy, I turned to Pita and smiled, and we winked at each other. That was an excellent greeting by Ginete standards. "You two must be here for a reason. Has a solution been found?"

"We are in the dark as much as you are," Teddy said. "We were invited to the Castle for dinner. There must be more going on than that, but you know we wouldn't miss a chance to come to see you."

"And have dinner," Zeid finished for him, with a twinkle in his eye.

"That, too," Teddy responded.

"Did you come through the tunnels?" I asked. The Whistle Pigs and Ginete have tunnels that traverse every area of the Kingdom of Zerenity, and they are always making more as needed. They travel up to the surface and back down using some kind of technology that always reminds me of Star Trek and the transporter room. Except since it only works from the surface to the tunnels and back, it is more like an elevator that makes the journey in a split second.

To use it, you stand on a circle of blue light and before you can blink you are either on the surface or back in the tunnels. The first time it happened to me, it scared the ziffer out of me. Now I love it. There is no other way to get into the tunnels, which makes them very secure because no one can see the circles unless the Whistle Pigs intend for them to be seen.

If Shatterskin had not shattered all of the landscape across his Kingdom, we could travel to him by tunnel. But the damage that Shatterskin caused didn't just happen on the surface. It shattered everything below for hundreds of feet. Every home of the Ginete and Whistle Pigs near Abbadon was destroyed at the very beginning of the fight against him, before I had been brought back from the Earth Realm and returned to Erda.

At first, no one could accept that the destruction was happening. Abbadon was destroying his own lands, the trees, and the animals that sustained the air and the environment. Why would he do that? In the end, it would mean his own destruction. It seemed insane, and the people of the Kingdom of Zerenity couldn't wrap their heads around that kind of crazy. Crazy behavior or not, he is still doing it. If we can't stop him, Abbadon will end up alone and on a barren planet, and he doesn't seem to care.

What could have possibly triggered this horrible behavior? What he is doing is inconceivable to all of us.

It would be easy to brush off what he is doing as the workings of a mad-man. His actions certainly appear that way. But everyone who met him as he lived undercover within the Kingdom of Zerenity said he gave off the appearance of a kind, well-mannered man.

For the most part, it has become impossible to convince most of the people that met him that he is a mass-murderer. But by selling the walking sticks infused with the deadly thought-worms, he had destroyed the lives of countless people. Thousands are dead.

He is always ahead of us. He always knows what we are doing. This is not the workings of a crazy man. Abbadon is deliberate and careful. To stop Abbadon, we have to out-think him and outmaneuver him.

So far we hadn't found a way to do that, and all of us are well aware that time is running out.

Eight

I could hear Earl's raucous laughter long before we reached the atrium. Sometimes I can smell rain when Earl is around, even when he is only Earl, not Coro, the commander of the storms. I suppose Earl's essence is the same as Coro's. In a way, it's like being a shapeshifter. Earl's wife, Ariel, commands the winds. I had never met them during the time they were in the Earth dimension, but my mother and father did. It had been a brief visit before Earl and Ariel returned permanently to Erda.

When I first met Earl and Ariel in Erda, Suzanne had introduced them as her mother and father. Since then I have heard rumors that they acted as mother and father when her birth parents took her sister, Meg, to another dimension, or maybe it was another planet, to keep her out of trouble.

The story was that Meg was too wild and free with her shapeshifter's abilities.

I never think of Suzanne as being lonely, she is always so busy taking care of all of us, but perhaps she misses them. I would understand that. I miss my Earth parents too. But both of us belong in Erda.

The fact that Earl and Ariel were at dinner meant something was up. But I knew that we never talked about problems while eating, so I tabled my urge to ask why they were there. Sooner or later I would find out. I was happy to wait because I knew it could end up being something that I wished I didn't know.

When Beru, Teddy, Pita and I had seated ourselves at the table, the metal toadstools hadn't delivered the food yet, and there were still four empty seats. I hoped that meant that Garth, Anne, Leif, and Sarah would be joining us. Even if we didn't talk about Abbadon at dinner, with Garth and Anne there, we might be treated to some interesting tales about dimension traveling.

It was Ruta who had brought Garth and Anne to our attention. Something to do with drinking in taverns and hearing them tell stories. I had seen what happened to Ruta when he drank. His drink of choice was some syrupy thing, and if he drank enough of it, he became a dancing block of wood. Admittedly, more than once, some of us had joined him as he danced on top of a table.

Leif and Sarah were another matter altogether. I had known the two of them in the Earth dimension. Both of them had been living there to keep an eye on me. The funny thing is, they hadn't remembered who they were any more than I did. But instinct took over, and they watched over me anyway. Now that both of them had also returned to Erda, they had also returned to their true selves.

Sarah is the oracle. She teaches, guides, and answers questions. Pretty much what she did in the Earth Realm, but in Erda she uses more magic. Leif is a wizard, and he looks exactly how I used to think wizards would look when I imagined them as a child. Except he dresses like the rest of us: no flowing robes or long gray beard. If we were in the Earth dimension, he could walk down the street and easily blend into the crowd.

However, he does have a magical staff which he sometimes uses. Once I asked him if he needed a staff to do magic, or was it just theater. Typically, Leif just smiled and asked me what I thought, which makes me believe that it's theater. It's what people expect for a wizard—a magical staff. I admit I like seeing it too.

Sometimes Leif and Sarah aren't people at all. Leif appears as a blue haze and Sarah as a blue light. They also appear when and where they want to, seemingly just by thinking about it. Tonight they walked into the atrium looking just like the people I knew back in Earth. Anne and Garth were with them looking a little confused, but our happiness at seeing them was evident and it didn't take long for them to join in the conversation.

I was right. We heard some interesting stories from them about other dimensions. When I asked them if they were always dimension travelers they looked at each other before answering.

"It's not that we don't want to answer you," Anne said, "It's that we don't know."

When everyone started asking them all at once why they didn't know, Garth held up his hand to stop the questioning.

"We would love answers, too. But we don't have them. We don't have a memory of ourselves as anything but this. I know Anne is my sister. I know we travel to different dimensions and gather stories. We try to keep out of trouble and remain as invisible as possible when we do so. But how we came to be this, we don't remember."

"Do you think you forgot when you were in another dimension, or someone or something made you forget?" Aki asked.

"That's something we have considered. Maybe we don't even belong in this one, and we have forgotten where we come from," Anne said.

"We both decided to live as much in the present as possible. At least as much as dimension traveling can be in the present."

Everyone laughed at that, because we all understood, to some small degree, that dimension traveling is also time traveling.

After that, the talk turned to things like the weather, or what new flower was blooming in the atrium garden. As I listened and looked around the table, I marveled at the diversity. No one thought anything of it.

My eyes stopped at Anne and Garth, the newcomers at our table. If they were living in the Earth Realm, they looked like they could have come from Ireland with their red hair and blue eyes. I caught Aki looking at me, and back to them. I wondered if she was thinking that too.

The table was full of beautiful beings, all so different, enjoying each other without any hint of separation or animosity. Sure, we teased each other, and sometimes I stamped my foot in frustration, but my heart was full of love for everyone there.

I embraced that feeling within every pore of my being because I knew that since all of us were there, it was almost time to leave. How we were going was a mystery, but I was sure this was one of those last suppers before everything changed.

Zeid reached under the table and held my hand. Just as I knew Earl and Ariel, Leif and Sarah, and I suspected Professor Link and Aki were doing. We were memorizing this moment, just in case we never had one like it again.

Nine

No one was surprised when Earl told us all to get some sleep and meet in the planning room the next morning at sunrise. He suggested that we keep our conjectures as to what we were doing to a minimum.

Both Beru and Zeid walked me to my room. Beru slipped off while Zeid paused with me outside my door. We had an unspoken agreement to keep our romantic feelings in the background until the battle with Abbadon was over, but that didn't stop us taking that extra moment to reassure each other that everything would work out.

We leaned into each other for a moment, and then I backed away and slipped into my room. After I closed the door, I stood there for a moment wishing I could reopen the door and invite Zeid in, but everything told me it would be unwise and selfish. I needed to be thinking of the mission and the good of the team, not myself.

A few hours later I was still struggling, trying to sleep, when I heard a familiar voice in my head, I was delighted. It only took me a few minutes to slip on my shoes. I hadn't undressed. Perhaps somewhere inside of me I knew that he would be coming to see me.

The Castle was quiet, but the hallways were lit with soft light so I could see where I was going. It was still a marvel to me that the trees provided everything that the people of Erda needed for energy. The roots of the trees were the source of the light that emanated from the walls. There was no need for light fixtures. The light was everywhere when we needed it.

I used the same door that we had let the rabbits out of just a few hours before. Outside, a full moon bathed everything with a blue-gold light making it easy to see where I was going.

Cahir said that they would be under the spreading oak that lived just outside the Castle walls. Even though I could see where I was going, I still tripped over my own feet as I rushed over to hug Cahir and see the family that he had brought with him. Cahir is a gray wolf that has been my companion for as long as I can remember. He doesn't like to be inside of castles or buildings, or Sound Bubbles, or use the circles of the Whistle Pigs. If he has to, he will, but the howl he makes while doing so is horrifying.

Cahir had been visiting his family. I was surprised but delighted that he had brought them with him.

"Oh, Cahir these pups are so precious."

I lay down on the ground and let them crawl all over me. It was only then that I realized that Cahir was there with just his children. "Where is your wife, Cahir?"

He hung his head as he pushed the answer into my head. "She is with our relatives in the great beyond."

"Oh, no. I'm so sorry."

I wrapped my arms around his neck and buried my face in his fur. Cahir lay down, and I lay with him, the pups walking over both of us as I mourned his loss with him.

"Did you bring your children here to be taken care of while we travel to Abbadon?"

"No, I brought them so you can see them before you travel."

"You won't be going with me?" I shrieked. I know I shouldn't have reacted, I should have immediately understood. But, Cahir was my eyes, my companion. I couldn't imagine going anywhere without him.

"Where you are going, I can't follow, Kara Beth."

I pleaded with Cahir to tell me more, but he wouldn't. I fell asleep out there lying on Cahir, his children snuggled up beside me. In the morning as the first rays of the sun began to lighten the sky, I awoke. Alone.

Beru found me there, crying, cold, and dirty.

"Get up. Now!" she barked.

Looking at my tear-stained face, she softened for a second and then brought herself back to giving orders. Little flower girl Beru was someone to be reckoned with. "You can't afford to do this, Kara, and if Cahir saw you now, he would not be proud of you."

I stamped my foot. And then stopped. I knew she was right. I sighed and followed Beru back to my room, trying to let Cahir's leaving be okay with me. I had only a few minutes to get cleaned up and get to the planning room. I didn't know who would be running the meeting, but it didn't matter. Being late was never, ever, an option. Unless you were trapped somewhere, and that may not even be a good excuse.

For once I was glad that there were no mirrors in Erda. People believed that Abbadon used them to see what we were doing. I wondered if they were right, or if it was a story they believed, a version of Snow White, where the wicked queen watched Snow White in a mirror so she could plan how to get rid of her.

Either way, we didn't have any, and for once I was glad. I didn't want to see what I looked like because if it was what I felt like, I was sure I would scare even myself.

A fast shower, clean clothes which once again lay magically on my bed, and a quick brush through my hair and I ran down the hall to the room, opening the door as the first ray of light hit the window and beamed its warm glow across the room.

Zeid rolled his eyes, Aki shook her head, and the three Priscillas started to laugh. Beru patted the seat beside her, and I slid in as gracefully as is possible for me.

It was Leif running the meeting. He didn't need to say anything. Everyone knew I had made it with only a second to spare. Food and drink were in the middle of the table. I pretended that I hadn't run the whole way and helped myself to a sweet roll, coffee, and some sliced mango.

Whatever was going to happen, I wanted to be well fed first. I guess I had left that thought channel open because everyone started to laugh. Well, not everyone. But I swear Ruta winked at me, and that made everything all right.

Ten

Looking at Leif sitting with Anne and Garth I figured it out. Suddenly it was clear what the plan was going to be. And as usual, I couldn't control myself. I blurted out the question, "Did you know this all along?"

Before Leif could say anything, I added, "Oh, that's what Cahir meant when he said he couldn't go with me."

"Yes, to both, Kara. We suspected this was going to be the answer, which is why we brought Anne and Garth here. And yes, Cahir was ahead of us all."

"Wait," Teddy said. "I'm lost here. What are you talking about?"

I looked at Teddy and said, "We can't defeat Abbadon now. The only way to do it is to stop him before he starts."

If I could see through his fur, I'm sure Teddy would have turned pale.

"Are you telling us that somehow we can go back in time? And back in time, we can stop Abbadon before he begins to destroy everything? How is that possible?"

Leif looked over at Professor Link who took over. "Technically we do it all the time with the Sound Bubbles, and portals, and even those of you who can teleport. All of these use a form of time manipulation. Well, that probably isn't the right word, but it's close.

"The portals open in different dimensions and different times, but they do it in a way that allows us to travel between these time zones without changing who we are in each. The way it works isn't as important as the fact that we already know how to do it.

"However, instead of sending you to another dimension we are going to send you to another time."

"So you knew about this too?" Zeid asked Link.

"I knew it was a solution if we didn't come up with another one. But it was Suzanne who came up with the idea. She talked it over with Leif and Sarah, and then brought it to me as a possibility."

I asked the next obvious question, trying to sound positive while feeling negative. "The fact that this seems like a simple solution means it's not, right? I mean, it sounds like we simply hop into some kind of time portal, find Abbadon, do something to make sure he doesn't start destroying everything, then hop back into the portal and return to this time when everything will be just hunky dory."

"Hunky dory? That must be something you learned in the Earth Realm, Pretty Girl," Teddy said.

"Yepper!"

Everyone laughed. It wasn't that funny, but we all needed some comic relief.

Link actually smiled at us and then did his famous squint before answering. "Yes, it sounds easy. And it would be wonderful if it could be just hunky dory as you said. But it's not quite that simple, as you have guessed.

"We have to be sure that you go back far enough. We don't know what caused the change. That in itself could be dangerous because whatever it was, doesn't want you to interfere with it. You could run into yourself while you are back there, and finally, if nothing does go wrong while you are there, what happens when you come back to this time? Will it be what it is now? Will you have changed something so drastically that some of us aren't here anymore? There are so many things that could be different. And, even if nothing has changed other than the planet isn't being destroyed by Abbadon, what if we don't get you back to the right time? The ramifications of that are something we can barely understand."

"Well, when you put it that way …," I said, and we all laughed again.

Professor Link waited until we had calmed down before speaking. "This is why we wanted you to be sure that there are no other solutions. This is a drastic one."

Zeid had been sitting quietly while we discussed the plan. He had barely moved and hadn't participated in any of the laughter. I knew that his thoughts were further along in what the consequences of this action could be than any of the rest of us. So when he asked the next question, I wasn't surprised.

"I think we all can see that this is the only way we can stop Abbadon, and save our Kingdom. If we do it right, it will restore it to what it was. People who died, won't have died. That would make it more than a victory. It would be healing."

Leif and Sarah smiled at him and nodded at him to continue.

"Obviously this will be an incredibly dangerous mission, so have you worked out who is going?"

"Aren't we all going?" I blurted out.

When no one answered me, I knew that we weren't. "Why not?"

Ruta grunted, and Beru reached out and held his hand.

"Okay, so everyone understands this but me?"

"If we all go, Suzanne said, "Then there is nobody here in this time frame who remembers who we are or where we went. Somebody has to stay, hold the memories, and be the marker that we can find again. And if the mission is not successful, we will need people here that can try to stop Abbadon as he continues in his quest to destroy Erda."

It was so obvious I felt stupid, but I kept on going, "Then who is going, and who is staying?"

This time it was Sarah who answered me.

"That, Kara, is the next decision, and much of it will be determined by where each of us will be of the most use, back in time, or here. However, that has to come after each of you thinks about the ramifications of going back in time.

"Is this something you could do if needed? No one is going to think less of you if you can't. It can't be about ego. It has to be about the team and what will work.

"If you go to the atrium, you'll find a bag of food for each of you to take while you do what you need to do to make this decision. You all have your own personal process for figuring things out. Just remember, even if you do decide that you want to be one of the ones that will go back in time, that still may not be the place for you. All you are doing now is examining if you would be willing. See you back here in a few hours."

No one said anything as we filed out of the room. Although we walked back to the atrium together, we remained silent, respecting that everyone needed to think this through for themselves. I knew that Sarah had asked us to think about it, but I already knew my answer. I was leaving. Cahir had told me the night before. I just hadn't understood what he meant. Now I did.

Eleven

Even though I knew the decision had already been made for me, I wanted to take some quiet time before we met again. I think that was Sarah's plan all along. Make sure we had food so we could go anywhere and give us each the space to come to terms with our decisions. There was no doubt in my mind that everyone would be saying yes to traveling in time. If we didn't, then with Abbadon on the move again, it was very possible we wouldn't be able to stop him this time.

My first thought was to go to the meditation room in the Castle. The Whistle Pigs always make a meditation space in their villages in the tunnels, and I often go into that quiet place when I am troubled. It was in one of those meditation rooms that I had first discovered that Sarah was the Oracle.

The meditation room in the Castle was the opposite of the ones in the Whistle Pig's tunnels. Although small and comfortable, it looked out into an enclosed garden. Because there were no curtains on the windows, the room changed with the seasons and the changing light of the day.

It was Leif who had shown me the room. He told me that it was one of my mother's favorite spaces and that she was the one who had designed the garden, planting it herself. No matter what the season, the garden was always beautiful.

My mother had made sure there were birdhouses scattered throughout the garden, and watching the birds choose their homes and then build their nests, taking one little piece of building material at a time, always calmed me down. If those little birds could be so patient and accomplish so much one tiny step at a time, I figured that I had a chance.

But today I needed to be out in the woods. I used the door in the training yard again. After Abbadon started his reign of destruction, that door had been bolted and continuously guarded. Since we had removed Deadsweep from the Kingdom, the Castle returned to its open door policy.

Yes, there was always a guard in the courtyard, but anyone could come and go as they pleased. The guard was only a precaution. No one believed that Abbadon would be returning through the garden gate. If he wanted to, he could probably blast the Castle and the nearby town of Dalry out of existence with a flick of his wrist. No, he liked toying with us just a bit too much.

The place I chose was not far from where I had woken up that morning. It was a grove of trees by a stream. I knew that if I followed the stream through the woods, I would eventually get to Dalry, but where I was heading was much closer. Cahir had shown it to me, and even though I knew he wasn't there, I wanted to see it again.

The grove of trees had arranged themselves so that there was a little open meadow between them. A rock lived in the center that was big enough to lie on and stare at the clouds going by in the sky. Today, the trees gave me a break and kept their limbs above my head and the roots in the ground. If it were a training day, that wouldn't have been the case.

Before lying on the rock, I walked around the circle of

trees and gave them each a pat or a hug. I wondered if when we went back in time, I would see them as small trees. I guess it depended on how far back we were going. I knew if we returned, the trees and everyone else would have barely missed us. We were the ones who would be missing everything we knew.

In Erda, everyone understood that all living things are sentient beings. In the Earth Realm, some people were beginning to learn that truth. But in Erda nature had always been treated as a partner instead of something to dominate. Wondering what could have caused Abbadon to turn so thoroughly against life, I lay back on the rock and fell asleep.

Zeid found me there a few hours later. The sun was no longer directly overhead, and a deer was eating the lunch I had never gotten around to eating. Both of us watched the deer finish my food. When she was done, she nodded to us and strolled off into the trees, only stopping for a moment to give us one last look. Did she know we were leaving?

"How did you know I was here?"

"Just followed your trail," Zeid laughed. "And I remembered that you used to like coming here when we were little. Cahir brought you back here when you didn't remember it."

"Do you think I will ever recover all of my memories?"

"Does it matter?"

Zeid sat with me on the rock as I pondered that question. Did it matter? Or was memory something that would return when I needed it? And perhaps without it, I was free to rediscover things.

"That's an interesting way to look it, Kara."

Neither of us had spoken out loud. Telepathy between the two of us had become comfortable and second nature.

A wind whooshed through the trees, and we looked up to see

Lady circling the clearing above our head. It was Suzanne's way of letting us know that it was time to return to the Castle.

On the way back, we held hands as if we were just two people enjoying a beautiful late summer's day. Not a princess or a future Queen and King. Not two people who were getting ready to leave behind the world that they knew. We were both choosing to be carefree for a few minutes more, taking in everything about the beautiful day to hold as a memory that might bring us back home. Because once we were called to do what needed to be done, I knew that we would do it together. Zeid would choose to be by my side no matter what I decided.

However, I was sure that he was aware that the choice had already been made for me, which meant it was chosen for him too. With one last glance back at the woods, Zeid opened the door in the wall, and we were on our way to our next adventure.

Twelve

We were the last ones to arrive at the meeting room, but no one was seated yet. Everyone was milling around and talking. It looked like one of the parties my parents would have at their home in the Earth dimension. However, a somber thread underlay the chatting and laughing.

As soon as Sarah saw us, she called the meeting to order. She didn't do anything that I could see, but I felt it, and I knew everyone else in the room did too.

The Priscillas who had so sweetly left me to myself to think things through flew to my shoulders and stayed there. No hair pulling this time. Zeid sat on one side of me, and Beru sat on the other. Across the table, Professor Link, Aki, and Niko stared at me. My teachers. I wondered what they saw. Did they think I could do it? Did they think that if I failed it would be their fault? They had to know I would never let them down. I am often an idiot, not the magical mage they probably hoped I would be, and often a clumsy person, but I am determined and that counted for a lot. Aki smiled. She knew. My gratitude for the three of them rose up and almost overwhelmed me. Now was not the time to get sentimental.

Ruta was on the other side of Beru. I wondered what they

had decided. I thought Beru would go with me, but did that mean Ruta would too? Anne and Garth sat beside Suzanne.

Earl and Ariel were not there. I knew they were letting us decide, and they would support us if we needed them. Teddy and Pita sat beside each other too. Whatever happened, they would work as a team, either here or there.

Once everyone was settled, Leif stood. "Before you give us your answers, let's pause and let the power of this moment infuse each of our spirits. Nothing you choose will be wrong. Together we will restore the peace and harmony to Erda."

"So say we all," sounded throughout the room. I knew that was for me. I loved that saying. It was Amen and So Be It wrapped up into one.

Leif looked around the room. "I see that all of you are willing to go." A chorus of nods was his answer. No one was surprised that he already knew. There was no need for a physical vote. He had read our decisions, probably before we were even aware of them.

"But not all of us can go. As we said, some of us must remain here in case the Back-In-Time team does not succeed. Of course, we believe that you will, but we can't leave the Kingdom undefended in case something goes wrong, or the BIT Team is not able to stop Abbadon immediately. The timing may not be perfect.

"Plus there are those that need to stay to maintain the time portal and provide a time anchor for the rest of the team. Which means partnerships may be broken up."

"Why?" Ruta grunted. We all knew why he asked. He and Beru were a partnership, and in spite of his logical exterior his heart was huge, and mostly belonged to Beru.

"For the very reason you don't like the idea, Ruta."

"It will be like a beacon in time, won't it?" Aki said.

Ruta nodded in understanding, and for a moment fear gripped my heart. Did that mean that Zeid would not be going with me? I understood about the beacon, but I wasn't sure I could do it without him. In fact, I wasn't sure that I could do it without all of them. For the first time, I realized how afraid I was.

"Who's deciding?" I blurted out trying not to sound as desperate as I felt.

"You all are," Leif said. He called his staff to one hand and reached out the other to Sarah, and the two of them left the room.

Those of us who were left stared at each other. Finally, Niko spoke, and we all sighed in relief. We were used to having Niko lead us.

"If we were planning a normal mission, Link would stay here. Do you all think this is true for this one?" A sound of approval went around the room. I thought I saw the Professor sigh and sink into his chair. Did this make him happy or sad?

"Since we need someone skilled at portals on both sides of the entrance, Garth and Anne would go, and Suzanne would stay. I assume this is something the three of you have already been working on?"

They nodded, and Niko continued. "Since Pita and Teddy provide the underground rooms, and Pita's brothers will stay here, and Teddy has a team that can stay, I am assuming it would be good to send both of them."

It was weird to see Teddy and Pita do a high five together. But I was glad they were both going. More than once we had to stay in their underground homes, and use their tunnels, and knew we would need them again. Without them, I wasn't sure how we were going to talk to the Whistle Pigs or Ginete that hadn't met us before. Or something. When I tried to think that through it didn't quite make sense, but still, I was happy they were coming.

Niko continued, "I think we need to send Ruta. He will be able to work with the trees more than any of the rest of us."

"Does that mean that Beru will stay here?" I squeaked.

Beru reached out and held my hand and Ruta's. "It's alright. If I stay, I can make sure you both return home."

Beru turned to Niko and said, "Because of course, Kara is going."

Niko nodded. "Thank you Beru for understanding. You will be invaluable here. Aki needs to go too." Niko glanced over at Professor Link who lowered his head but nodded in agreement.

"Aki has skills and knowledge that none of the rest of us have."

Zeid spoke up. "That leaves the Priscillas and me. There is no way I am not going. There are plenty of heart beacons remaining here to bring us home. My place is beside Kara."

"Ours too," squealed the Priscillas as they clutched my hair as if someone was going to pull them away right at that moment.

It was the most inappropriate time to burst into tears, but that is what I did. I think I cried for everyone because there was not anyone who didn't look as if they didn't want to start crying.

A few minutes later, after we all composed ourselves. Leif and Sarah came back into the room.

"It's decided, then," he said. "Well done. Now, it's time to plan."

Thirteen

The first question that we had to answer was how far back in time we would go. It was possible that Abbadon only started changing a few years ago, but on the other hand, what if it was hundreds of years before and no one noticed. How would we figure out when it had started?

It was the most critical question that we had because if we didn't go back far enough, then it might still be too late to stop him. If we went too far, then the trigger point would be in the future, and we wouldn't be able to affect the outcome at all.

After much debate, we decided it was better not to go too far into the past. If we ended up in time after Abbadon had started his reign of destruction, at least we would have a better chance of stopping him than we did in the current time frame when he had gathered so much power. After much discussion, we decided on two hundred years into the past.

Our next decision involved where we would go. We had to be careful not to step out of a portal where Abbadon could see it. We were afraid that he might use it to travel in time too. Or perhaps to travel to Zerenity without being seen.

Zeid asked if that mattered since Abbadon seemed to be able to go anywhere he wanted to without being seen anyway.

Suzanne said that was a good point, but we still needed to be careful. Besides we didn't want Abbadon to know that we were there. That was the whole point of doing it this way, he wouldn't see us coming.

Our first decision was to put our end of the time portal in the woods outside the Castle walls. "If we are so close to the Castle, why not put it inside the Castle?" I asked.

"What if on your return the Castle isn't here, or no one knows who you are? Too many variables that we can't manage," Professor Link replied.

Everyone nodded in agreement. There were so many factors to take into consideration, including not knowing where Abbadon would be. What if he wasn't at his Castle when we got there?

"It seems as if we need more information about the past, and since there are people that lived then, why don't we ask them? In fact," I paused to think about what I was going to say next, "weren't you all here hundreds of years ago? I know I don't remember that time, but you must. What's going on here? Why are you acting like you don't know what the past was like?"

The more I talked, the more upset I got. "Are you all pulling my leg somehow? If we are only going back a few hundred years, that's nothing to some of you. Besides, we have libraries and people even older, like my father. Why are you all pretending that you don't know?"

By that time I was standing, and everyone was looking at me without any expression on their faces which made me angrier. I would have stomped my feet the way I did when I got angry, but Beru pinched my leg, and I stopped.

"Are you done?" Niko asked. When I reluctantly sat down because Beru pulled my tunic, Niko continued.

"Think it through just a little bit more, Kara Beth. Of

course, some of us remember hundreds of years ago, and yes we have libraries and historians. But, and this is a huge but, what if what we remember turns out not to be what happens because you have been there changing things? If we tell you what happens it might not happen.

"The smallest thing you do might mean that towns don't get built, or one of us has died, or … so many things could be different. If we tell you how it is because we remember it that way, we could be enabling a change that destroys everything even more than what Abbadon is planning."

I sat there taking in what Niko said. He was right of course, which is why I wasn't leading the team, he was. No one said anything as I thought through everything he had said, especially his last words. The implication of what he meant hit me as if I had been thrown into a pool of ice water.

"Wait. So we could make it worse by going back?"

"Yes."

"What if that is what Abbadon wants? What if he is counting on us to time travel? What if this is his plan all along. What if he is waiting for us and because of that everything is destroyed in a flash? Have you thought of that?"

I was standing again. I really had to stop being so melodramatic, but the implication of what we were going to do had just begun to make itself felt in me.

Leif and Sarah had been sitting quietly while we talked things through. As I stood trembling, Leif rose and addressed us all.

"Yes, what if? Thank you, Kara, for bringing it all out in the open so clearly."

I sat, and Leif continued. "Yes, all these things could be true. It's a chance we are taking. After hearing all the reasons why this might not work, does anyone want us to stop moving forward with the time travel idea?"

"I don't want to stop," Teddy said. His deep, calm voice filled the space and made me feel better. "But is there anything we can do to make it safer and mitigate the chances of us making it worse?"

Aki had been silent for most of the meeting. When I had begun to act up, she had watched me with those pale blue eyes that became darker as I spoke. When Teddy asked his question, she stood, or more accurately, she floated up.

She looked across the table at Niko and said, "Perhaps we should tell them now, brother?"

I think the whole room asked the question at the same time, "Brother?"

Fourteen

Niko held up his hand to stop the chatter. While I was shocked at the revelation, I was also not surprised. Something had always made me think that both of them were much more than met the eye.

"Before you ask, no, we have never told anyone our story before."

Niko glanced over at Sarah, and added, "Although I think at least one of you had figured it out and decided to wait for us to tell."

Sarah smiled at both of them, and Niko continued. "Yes, we are brother and sister. Yes, Kara Beth, I have heard you ask yourself if we were both more than what we appeared to be.

"Yes, we can change our forms, not as shapeshifters but as chameleons. Which means we don't become something else the way Suzanne becomes a dragon. We shift to fit into our environment. It's the same as your chameleons in the Earth Realm.

"We've kept this a secret to protect ourselves, and to protect the people that we have come to know and love."

Niko sighed and looked at his sister. "I think that Aki tells stories better than I do, so I'd like to turn this over to her."

Aki had remained standing while Niko spoke. "Yes, I'll tell

you the story. However, if you don't mind, I would prefer to do it in a more relaxed atmosphere. Perhaps in the garden in the atrium? In an hour? That will give Niko and me time to gather our thoughts."

As we rose to go, she added, "I feel that some of you are worried. Have we been spies all along? Are we preparing to leave you now? I promise you that neither of those two things is true. We are with you as fully as ever, and we will continue to fight beside you to stop Abbadon. We also have personal reasons, which we will share with you."

I turned to look at Aki who had taught me so much, and my heart broke for her. I walked over and put my arms around her. Aki hesitated, and then tentatively patted me on the back, whispered "Thank you," in my ear, and then she was gone, and I was left holding nothing.

"Someday I am going to have to learn how to do that myself," I mumbled to myself. Ruta snorted. It was the proper response.

That was never going to happen.

****

"So, what do you want to do while we wait for the story?" Beru asked me. As always, she had me pegged. I didn't just want to sit around, and I didn't want to spend time wondering about what would happen, or not happen. There was enough of that going on. I wanted to do something different. Something that would get my mind off of what we were going to learn, and where we were going to go.

"Since I won't be seeing you for a while once we leave, Beru, why don't you suggest something we can do together."

Beru stopped in the middle of the hallway and looked at me as if she was trying to decide what to say.

"Anything, Beru. Just tell me, I'll do it."

In our heads, we both heard Professor Link say, "It's on the way," and a few seconds later we heard the harmony of the Sound Bubble's hundreds of notes coming our way.

I didn't ask Beru where we were going, but I wasn't surprised when we landed in Kinver just a few minutes later. In fact, I was delighted. I love Kinver, Beru's village. Lorraine and Liza came running out of the house to greet us, and I could see James coming up the road.

"This is wonderful," James said as he ran the last few yards to us. "We weren't expecting you, so it makes it even more delightful."

I giggled and hugged James and his wife, Lorraine, and gave Liza a quick hug.

"We're only here for a minute," Beru said. "I wanted to leave something with you. It's a letter to my parents."

"In case they come back while you are gone?" Liza asked.

I looked at Beru. She wasn't going anywhere. Then I realized that Beru was making sure that in case something went wrong with the BIT team's trip, there would be a record somewhere that she had loved them. It was such a good idea I wondered why we all hadn't thought of that, but then perhaps everyone had, and it was just me that hadn't.

Lorraine took Beru off to write the letter, while I spent some time chatting with James and Liza. As casually as I could, I asked Liza how old she was. Liza replied that in Erda terms, she was a child still. That meant she wouldn't have been born yet where we were going.

"Would you leave a note in the past for me?"

"How do you know that's what we are doing?"

Then it dawned on me. Since Liza could see 4D, could she also see timelines? See what we call the past and the future?

Liza answered my unspoken thoughts. "You know that time is

fluid, don't you? Every choice means a different outcome. Many time-lines. So no, I don't know what is going to happen, or what did happen. I only know that you are leaving tomorrow for the past. What happens after that depends on what you find, and what you do—all of you.

"But we know your heart. Plus you have many skills and a team that travels with you that will not let the mission fail. We'll see you again. For us maybe tomorrow, maybe a few weeks, or even a year from now. But I know we'll see you again."

James looked at his daughter with pride. "If she says so, Hannah. It will be so."

I loved it when James and his family called me Hannah. And this time it reminded me that traveling between dimensions was something people did all the time. Time travel would not be that much different. Or at least I was counting on Liza's belief to make it so.

Fifteen

Aki and Niko were waiting for us in one of my favorite spaces in the atrium. The rose garden. There were roses of all kinds growing in what looked like wild abandon, but I knew it was careful planning. The scent of roses never left the air. We walked through the trellis that was invisible underneath the massive rose vine that covered it. It was large enough that even the tallest of us didn't have to duck beneath the blooms hanging down off the vines, but we all got a whiff of the pink blossoms as we passed under them.

There were benches set up in a small courtyard inside the garden. Niko and Aki were standing in front of their bench and nodded at each of us as we entered. They looked different. It was nothing that I could put my finger on, but something had shifted. Perhaps it was simply their relief that they didn't need to keep their secret anymore.

Once we settled down, Niko sat, and Aki remained standing.

"We were trying to decide if we should begin by telling you where we were a few hundred years ago, before we came to the Castle to serve the King and his family, or if we should begin by telling you what we can do. We decided to get the worst of it over first. Where we were."

Aki looked at Niko and received an encouraging nod. Now that I saw them together I could see the resemblance. On the other hand, did they actually look like what they were showing us, or were they in their chameleon disguise?

I remembered the first time I saw Aki I had the feeling that Aki could twist herself around and turn into a wisp of smoke, or slither across the floor without making a sound. She had flicked her long pale white hair into the air, and for a moment she had hung there just like a wisp of smoke, her blue eyes glowing, and then she had disappeared. It had been the first time I had ever seen someone do that and I thought I had imagined it.

Niko was darker, more substantial. Like a Greek statue. It was as if they were the opposites of the same idea.

My thoughts were interrupted when Aki said, "Until we came here, Niko and I were slaves in Abbadon's Castle."

I could hear the audible intake of breath as we took in what she had just said. Only Sarah and Leif stayed silent, but I could see a single tear moving down Sarah's cheek.

Once everyone had settled down again, Aki continued.

"Yes, it was as horrible as you can imagine. But for a long time, we didn't realize how awful it was. We had been slaves from the time we were children, and all we saw were other slaves of other "races" so it was all that we knew. There were no free beings in Abbadon's Castle.

"He was the master, and the rest of us did his bidding. And it was a cruel bidding. If any of us disobeyed or made a mistake, we were horribly punished. It almost always involved some form of whipping, which was the better choice, because otherwise, it was death in some painful way.

"What made it worse was that we had to whip each other while the others watched."

Aki started trembling, and Niko reached up and pulled her

down onto the bench next to him. He put his arm around her, and she continued.

"At each whipping and each gruesome death, Abbadon grew stronger. It was as if he lived off of the pain he inflicted—not just the physical pain, but also the emotional pain. However, when I was a child, I thought that because he cried during these punishments that he was sorry that it had to be done, and I felt sorry for him. I worked hard to always be perfect. Not only because I didn't want to be whipped, but because I wanted to please Abbadon and make him happy."

Aki turned and looked at Niko. "Niko was not so easily fooled. He knew that Abbadon was not crying because he was sad. He was crying from joy. It was a release for him."

Aki must have heard me begin to ask a question because she held up her hand. "I'll get to it, Kara."

"Niko tried to tell me that Abbadon was a monster, but I didn't want to believe it. However, I was good enough in Abbadon's eyes, so he never punished me. The story was different for Niko, as you can imagine. So he rebelled. Secretly he was training himself, and others. Because he often rebelled in ways that Abbadon noticed, he was often whipped. I kept trying to tell him that if he did what he was supposed to do, it wouldn't happen, and he kept trying to tell me that Abbadon was an evil monster.

"One day, Abbadon noticed me crying as Niko was being whipped and that was the end of my believing in Abbadon, because he had the guard bring the whip to me and made me beat my own brother. Abbadon told me that if I didn't whip him hard enough, he would kill him.

"Abbadon reminded me of the bodies I had seen hanging outside the Castle and told me that is what would happen to Niko. He would hang him there until he died. So I did what he said. I used the whip on my brother.

"When I was done whipping Niko, Abbadon rewarded me by whipping me himself."

We were all crying by then, and Sarah asked Aki if she wanted to stop. Aki took a shuttering breath and said, "I have to get through this."

After collecting herself, she continued, "That's when I joined Niko and trained with him and the few people he trusted. We had to continue to look weak and subservient, but we were all growing stronger and more flexible.

"Niko had a mentor. He was an old crippled man. He had never told us his real name, but we called him Hawk because he always seemed to know what was going on.

"We had been told that Hawk had been there since he was a young man and that he had allowed himself to age because he wanted to die and move on. At the time he could barely move, but he used to be a fighter, and it was Hawk who trained Niko and then watched over us as we trained. We had to make sure no one saw us in case they decided to turn us in to avoid their own punishments."

"A few months after I joined Niko, we heard a rumor that Abbadon had learned about the training and was searching for who it was. Hawk came up with a plan for us to escape.

"He did it knowing that once it was discovered that it was him who helped, he would die a long, painful death. He didn't care. Hawk said it was time to be free. He would go through the door called death, and we would go to someplace other than Abbadon's castle.

"We made him a promise. We would come for Abbadon one day. He told us he knew we would. He had already seen it. That night we escaped. It took us many months, but we made our way across the country, to Darius' Castle.

"The King took us in without question. And that is why we have to complete this mission. We will stop Abbadon. Hawk said we would. But only if we go."

Sixteen

A long silence fell over the garden. All that we could hear was the singing of the birds, and the water tumbling over the miniature waterfall on the other side of the atrium.

Niko kept his arm around his sister, and they waited. None of us moved. I was contemplating the horror of what we just heard and had no idea what to say, or do, to make it better, or at least how to comfort Aki. I never thought I would need to comfort her. She was always so strong and sure.

She and Niko were the ones who taught us how to be fighters. Now I understood why, and how much it had cost them to learn what they knew.

The Priscillas had been quiet, Pris and Cil on my shoulders and La on Zeid's. Without saying anything, the three of them flew over to Aki and landed in her hair. Ever so gently they started to run their fingers through her long, pale white hair while whispering something that none of us could hear.

As they combed and whispered, I thought I heard a little melody and I realized that they were singing. Niko was staring at them as Aki closed her eyes and let the tears run down her cheeks.

Still, no one spoke. The Priscillas sang louder. I didn't know the song, but obviously, Niko and Aki did. Niko had turned almost as white as his sister. Finally, he whispered in a hoarse voice, "Where did you learn that song?"

It was Sarah who answered him as the Priscillas continued to comb and sing. We could see Niko's color return, and the grip on his sister's hand loosen.

"They learned it where you did, Niko."

"But I don't remember learning it. Only the song feels so familiar, as if someone used to sing it to me."

Because I had unconsciously unfocused my eyes so that I was close to seeing the world in 4D, I saw the little blue light leave Sarah and hover over Niko.

He stopped breathing for a moment, and when his breath came rushing out the words came out too: "Our mother used to sing it to us."

****

The Priscillas moved to Aki's and Niko's shoulders, and waited, as did the rest of us. Finally, I realized that everyone was waiting for me, because wasn't I always the one with the questions?

"Your mother? Where is your mother? Was she a slave in Abbadon's Castle too? Is she still alive? What do you remember? How long has it been since you have seen her?

"Sorry, I know that is a long list of questions, but I thought I would get it all out into the open so that you wouldn't have me interrupting you over and over again."

"You have an interesting way of being courageous, little one," Aki said, smiling at me. The Priscillas had brought her back to herself, and she looked even more beautiful than before if that was at all possible. Sometimes I didn't resent being called little one, and this was one of those times.

"How could you call me courageous? You are the ones who have endured hardships. I only ask questions and fall over things."

Aki laughed. "It takes courage to ask questions, too. So yes, you deserve an answer. Niko remembers more than I do though. I was very young when Abbadon's Raiders took us."

I drew in my breath. I had an idea that was what happened, but to hear it made it real.

Niko looked at Aki, who nodded at him, and he took up the story.

"No, our mother was not a slave in the Castle. We don't know about our father. Perhaps our mother would have told us one day, but she never had a chance. We were both taken from our village when we were very young and have never seen our mother since.

"She may have died that day. It is something that we may never know. Abbadon's raiders stormed the village and took only the children. Abbadon liked training the young.

"Once we became slaves, he did his best to beat every bit of our memories of our past lives out of us. But that song brought back some of those memories.

"Which means that we get to ask you, Pris, where the three of you learned it."

It was Cil who answered. "A long time ago we visited your village and heard the women singing that song. Long before you and your mother."

I burst out without thinking, "Great Zut, how old are you three anyway?"

All three laughed, but it was Pris who said, "From the beginning."

"What beginning?"

"The beginning of the story!"

"What story?" I asked through clenched teeth. Couldn't they give more than a brief answer?

"I know what story they mean," Aki said. "And so do you."

"The two bored brothers on the space ship? Are you serious? That wasn't a made up story?"

Four people shook their heads no. Leif, Sarah, Aki, and Niko.

"So those brothers could be responsible for this mess?"

"It's possible," Niko said, back in control. "But now that you have heard what we had to tell you, it seems obvious where and when we are going back to in time."

"Your village? Before your capture?" I hazarded a guess.

Finally, I understood why Aki and Niko had to tell us their secret. They knew Abbadon. They knew his Castle.

I had one last question.

"Didn't Abbadon recognize you when he was here? Or why didn't you recognize him?"

"We never saw him. We should have, and that's a failing on our part. And if he saw us, he would never have recognized us either," Niko said, as he let go of the look he was holding and became his true self.

Seventeen

I couldn't help it. I gasped, and my mouth fell open. Aki just looked at all of us and started laughing, and became herself, too. Aki and Niko didn't stay in their true forms for long. They waited for a beat and then shifted back. I suppose that was a good idea because otherwise, we might not have been able to keep our attention on our planning.

"Well." Professor Link said. "That was interesting."

His timing was perfect. Everyone began to laugh, including Niko and Aki. We laughed so hard tears ran down our faces. It was a relief to let it all go, especially after hearing the horror story that had been Niko and Aki's life.

Trying to be serious, Link said, "I see why he didn't know you ..." and we all started laughing again.

Finally, we ran out of steam and turned our attention back to Professor Link. If he was upset that Aki wasn't exactly the woman he thought she was, to his credit he didn't show it.

I wasn't so sure I would be so calm if Zeid turned out to look like another being. For a brief moment, I had the horrible thought that perhaps that was possible and I turned to look at him.

He must have known what I was thinking and that I was

going to turn because he was looking directly at me making a silly face. "Stop it," I hissed, even though I wanted to start laughing again.

Luckily no one was looking except the Priscillas, and of course, they joined in on the tease and made a few silly faces of their own, making sure that their backs were to the rest of the team so that it was only me who had to work at not laughing.

Finally, I pulled myself together enough to hear Link say, "Now that we know the time and where to send the BIT team, there are a few other things to put into place. But I think we can work those kinks out this afternoon. Which means you will all be able to leave in the morning."

Sarah stood and gestured towards the other side of the atrium. "Then I think this is the perfect time for a break. It looks as if lunch is ready. I suggest we eat and then meet again back in the planning room."

Something had changed in that rose garden. We had heard the story of Aki and Niko, and we had seen their true form. But it wasn't seeing them as themselves that had changed things. It was that a secret was revealed and we all felt lighter for it.

I watched Niko and Aki walk out of the garden heading towards lunch and could feel their joy that they were no longer hiding. Maybe it was something else too. They were going home. What they would find none of us knew, but they were going to go back and take us with them.

****

"Can we leave ourselves notes? Literal notes from our future self written by our present self to our past self? Or if we are in the past, we would be present then, too? Either way, can we leave ourselves notes?"

That was me, trying to work things out by speaking them out loud.

"Wait. It would be the other way around, wouldn't it? We could agree where the BIT team would put messages, and then you, still here in the future present, could find them. That is if we don't change too many things and you are all still here to find them.

"Ziffer, this time travel stuff is confusing. Am I the only confused one?"

Professor Link didn't make one of his squinty faces at me when he answered, so I wasn't sure if the questions were stupid or not.

"No, you're not the only one. It is confusing. But as far as we know, you could leave us messages. We could agree as to where, but it won't do as much good as you might think. Because if nothing changes we couldn't get your messages in the dead zone, which is where you will be traveling, without Abbadon seeing us."

"Well, we have an idea," Garth said. "Anne and I could go back and forth."

"No," Link said. "Much too dangerous, both for you two, and everyone else. Every trip through the time portal could change something.

"No, we will have to trust that each team is doing their part. Those of us who stay here will have to remain constantly alert, looking for things that are changing and dealing with them as they come up.

"As we have discussed, for us it will feel as if you have only been gone a short time. Depending on how long it takes you to stop Abbadon, it could be a few hours or a few weeks.

"For those of you traveling in time, it will be longer. Take your time. Don't think that you have to be done within a particular time frame to protect us. Be cautious, but also don't be afraid to do what you need to do to stop him."

"What can we take with us?" I asked. "When I came through the portal between dimensions I could only bring what I was wearing. Is this true for the time-portal too? Does that include what we are carrying, like a walking stick?"

"Or food?" Zeid added. "Or supplies? Can we bring them?"

"We'll prepare them. And you'll be carrying the supplies, but we don't know if they will end up back there with you or not," Professor Link said.

Suzanne stepped in, "I wish we knew more. Dimension traveling and back in time travel should be a very similar experience, but we won't know for sure until you try it. However, you have all faced unknowns many times and figured it out as you went along. I know that every one of us trusts that you know enough to do this.

"Even though you won't be able to communicate with us, you will be able to communicate with each other. You know how tricky Abbadon can be. Stay alert. You'll be fine."

It felt as if Suzanne was talking to confirm to herself that all would be fine. It was the first mission we had gone on without the whole team.

I had to ask one last question of the team that was staying behind. "Do any of you remember seeing us before? Like a long time ago, when you were younger?"

I hadn't seen Earl standing in the doorway when I asked the question. I was surprised. It was hard to miss Earl when he came around, even when he wasn't being Coro. This time, though, he had slipped in without anyone noticing until he laughed, sending a swirl of wind around the room.

"Ha. I told you she would ask that question," Earl roared.

"Yes, little one. Some of us remember you. But if we tell you what we remember…well, I think you can see the problem.

"All we can do is reassure you that all of you working together are wiser than Abbadon and all his minions.

"I know you want to ask more questions, little one, but we have no more answers."

Leif stood, called his staff to his hand and said, "Once again, I suggest rest. Tomorrow you are leaving at sunrise on your great adventure."

With that, he and Sarah blinked out and the rest of us stood around looking confused.

After all the talking and planning, there was nothing more to do, except do what he told us to do and show up in the morning.

Eighteen

Beru walked me to my room as she often did, and we stood there trying to say something that would make it better for both of us. I had no idea how I was going to leave and be without her.

From the moment I had stepped through the portal from the Earth dimension into Erda, she had been there. Sometimes even when I hadn't realized she was watching over me, she was. She pinched, laughed, made faces, dragged me to training, and took care of me afterward. Beru made everything about life better. She and I were sisters.

The only thing that was making leaving a little bit easier was thinking that what we were doing might change her world for the better. Perhaps she would find her parents again.

But I knew I wasn't the only one that she would be missing. Ruta would be with me and not with her. Beru and Ruta were inseparable. She thought of Ruta as her brother. They were each other's families. Perhaps we would be able to restore his family, too. If it could be done, I would.

"Are you going to lock me in my room tonight, Beru," I teased. "I never did understand why you used to do that."

"Well, it won't do me any good to lock you in anymore since

you can unlock everything now with a flick of your wrist."

Beru paused and flashed a smile, "I did it that first night to tease you. I had heard you knew how to unlock doors, so I thought you would be out in a flash. When you didn't come out, I was surprised. But I didn't want to go back on what I had done. Then Aki told me to keep locking you in until you remembered what you already knew."

"It worked, didn't it? Thank you, Beru for always taking such good care of me."

We hugged, and I cried. Hugging Beru always felt like hugging a beautiful flower. A strong, confident flower.

Beru pulled back from the hug, and I could see tears in her eyes. She gave me a gentle push into my room.

"Go sleep. Who knows when you will find a bed again," she said, and then turned and walked away.

My feelings weren't hurt. I knew Beru was trying to be brave for both of us. That's what she always did.

I loved my room at the Castle. It had the perfect amount of light if I was in my room during the day, which wasn't often. The bed was cozy and warm, or cool depending on the season.

Although there was very little in the room, it always felt as if it wrapped itself around me to keep me comfortable and safe. I hoped it would still be here if and when we returned.

At first, I couldn't sleep at all, but soon a blue haze settled over me, and I drifted away. But before I did, I thanked Leif for his help sleeping and for everything he had done for me as Hannah in the Earth dimension and Kara Beth in Erda. I didn't hear his promise that we would be safe. I felt it. I hoped he was right.

****

Morning found me wanting to say goodbye to everyone I could before meeting the team at the portal. First I found the metal toadstools in the atrium preparing the dining area for the day. I took the time to say thank you to each one. I called them all George, but when I reached the one I believed to be the George that always took care of me, I patted him on his metal tray balanced on the top of his head and said, "I appreciate all that you have done for me, George."

I knew it was him when he vibrated and did a little hop step. Perhaps Teddy had programmed this robot to do that just for me, but I always wanted to believe that since all things are living, that each of them was also a sentient being and he had figured it out for himself.

I grabbed a roll and a cup of coffee and wandered off back into the rose garden to wait for sunrise. I wasn't trying to spy on anyone, but Professor Link and Aki didn't know I was there when they appeared outside the garden. Once they started talking, I didn't know what to do. If I interrupted them, perhaps they wouldn't get to say goodbye, so I stayed silent.

It would have been a grownup thing for me to do not to listen, but then I'm not all that grownup, and I am perpetually curious, so I couldn't help myself.

Link and Aki were whispering, but I could hear them by blocking out every other sound. I couldn't see them directly, but I could see their shadows on the floor in front of me as the light from the dining area flooded over them.

"I should have told you," Aki said as she leaned forward putting her forehead on Link's chest.

Link rubbed her back to comfort her and then lifted her chin so he was looking down into her eyes. "It doesn't change anything, Aki. What you look like is not who you or any of us are. After all, none of us are what we appear to be."

"You are," Aki whispered.

"No, Aki, I too am not exactly as I appear. Just as none of the beings that we know are their forms, we are all more than can be seen with the eyes. I love the essence of you. Yes, you have made this form appealing to the human in me. But I love you no matter what you look like."

"Tell me the truth, Seth. It didn't seem as if you were really shocked yesterday. Were you?"

"I wasn't, Aki. I already knew. Research is my work."

"And you loved me anyway?"

"I love you anyway. Come back to me, Aki. In whatever form you wish to be."

They stood together for another moment and then moved away.

I didn't move. Seth? I didn't know that was Link's real name, which wasn't the point. It was that Link knew much more than he ever told us. That didn't bother me at all. It made me feel more secure knowing that with all that he had researched, he thought that we could accomplish our mission. I realized that they all thought we could. And most of them knew more than they were saying.

It was a good thing. I was planning on holding on to it. And Aki and Link's secret. It was theirs to tell, and I would do my best to make sure that Aki returned to him. That we all returned to the ones we loved.

Nineteen

When I was sure that Link and Aki were gone, I slipped out of the garden and hurried to where I was supposed to be. Thankfully, I wasn't the last one to arrive. Everyone was still there milling around, looking a little lost.

Zeid was waiting for me, and I slipped up beside him and held his hand. The Priscillas were busy flitting from one person to the next. I wasn't sure if it was because they were nervous, excited, or both. I knew I was both. So nervous I was afraid I was going to chew my lip off, and so excited about the prospect of the new adventure that tingles were running the whole way up and down my body.

We were all standing just outside the Castle walls on the edge of the tree line. Only Link and Suzanne were there from the team that was staying. I knew Cahir was back in Eiddwen with his children, and Berta would take care of anything that he needed while I was gone. I thought about Berta and my father, and I hoped they would be there when we got back.

Looking around, I wondered where Leif, Sarah, Earl, and Ariel were. Maybe they didn't see any need to say goodbye. I didn't expect to see Beru. We had said our goodbyes the night before, and I didn't think she wanted to break down in front of anyone any more than I did.

I glanced over at Ruta standing by himself at the edge of the group looking more forlorn then I had ever seen him look before. For a moment I thought of walking over to him, but a glance from him in my direction warned me off. He needed to deal with what was going on with him in his own way.

After checking who was there, I realized that we were waiting for Teddy and Pita. During our meeting, they had both remained very quiet, so I had no idea how they felt about leaving everything behind and moving into the past. Did they have a better idea of what they would find in their communities than we did?

Garth and Anne were standing with Suzanne talking in low voices. It was the three of them who were setting up the actual portal, and I wasn't sure if it was a good thing that they were still talking about it. Niko was pacing back and forth. I guessed he was trying to work off some energy. Aki came over and put her hand in his, and he calmed down. That was good. He was supposed to be our leader. No one wanted to see him nervous or afraid. At least I didn't. I had enough of that going on myself.

Just when I started wondering if we were going to have to go without them, I heard Teddy call out, "Hey ho, travelers!" and he and Pita came into view. Pita looked as if he had been running trying to keep up with Teddy, and Teddy was pushing a big cart filled with something. Teddy, as always, was calm and contained, as if we were only going on a simple pleasure trip.

"Sorry, we ran a little late working on these," he said, pulling out what turned out to be backpacks from the cart. He and Pita started to hand one to everyone, checking the names on them first.

"We tweaked these packs a bit so that they can travel with us. Each one is matched as closely as possible to the energy that your bodies give off, so it should easily go through the portal with you."

"How did you figure that out?" Aki asked.

"Well, we've been running transportation type things for a long time. You've probably never thought about the fact that when we travel to the surface or down to the tunnel with our transportation circles, you can bring anything you want with you.

"After you mentioned that you didn't know what would go through the portal with us, Pita and I realized that what we did with the transportation circle could probably work if we tweaked them in the same way with the time-portals.

"We solved the last of the problems late last night or early this morning, whichever way you look at it. Then Beru showed up, and with her help, we packed each one with what we thought you might need. Of course, there is water, and some food bars, along with extra clothes. Things like that."

By the time Teddy finished telling us what he, Pita, and Beru had been up to all night, we had our packs on. Mine was so comfortable I barely noticed that I was wearing it. Teddy saw me smiling, and added, "Yes, we made them to be comfortable based on who is wearing it. Even if we didn't have your names on it, you would know if you picked up the wrong pack and tried to wear it. Oh, Princess Toes, Beru put things for the Priscillas in your pack."

We all laughed as the Priscillas started twirling around in the air in celebration, followed by a sigh of relief knowing we had more supplies than we thought we would have.

"You two have done it again," Suzanne said, hugging them both.

Teddy bowed and said, "We aim to please."

As everyone moved closer to where the portal was going to

be, Teddy took my hand. "That little button I gave you before you went on your first mission? You know it won't work where we are going because you and this Castle will be in different time frames. But do me a favor, and leave it on anyway? You never know …"

"I'd do anything for you, Teddy, you know that," I said.

"It's time," Suzanne shouted. I'd never heard her yell like that before, but I knew it was essential that we left when the portal was ready. I felt the same way I did when I stepped through the portal to Erda, except this time I was holding Zeid's hand, and Teddy's huge paw was resting on my shoulder. Whatever happened, it was going to happen to us together.

Suzanne's familiar, "Go, go, go" was in my ears. We all took a deep breath and stepped through to the other side.

Twenty

If Zeid hadn't been holding my hand, I would have tripped and fallen on my face the same way I did the first time I came through a portal. Instead, this time, Zeid pulled my hand, and Teddy kept his grip on my shoulder. We all stepped out, or in my case, almost fell out, at nearly the same time. But it was Aki and Niko who floated out as if they had done it a million times.

This end of the time-portal had been placed to put us a few miles outside of Aki and Niko's village over two hundred years in the past. Which in Earth time would have been thousands of years. I think. The time exchange between dimensions was confusing enough and then add the back-in-time ingredient, and I was even more confused.

What we were trying to do was to arrive before the Raiders took Niko and Aki from the village. And this is where the whole thing was wonky. Were we going to stop the invaders from taking them? Would that mean that the Aki and Niko traveling with us would disappear from the team because they would become someone else?

Would they be able to see the children that they were? If we stood by and let Abbadon's Raiders take them, would we be guilty by not stopping them? These were the kinds of issues we had hashed over and over again back at the Castle and ended up deciding to go with what happened at the moment.

As soon as everyone was out of the portal, Niko held up his hand, and we gathered around.

"Take a good look around you. This is where the time-portal we hope to use to return to the future will be waiting for us. Suzanne said she would try to place others around Abbadon's kingdom, but it's dangerous. Someone else, like Abbadon, might see one and try to use it. This time-portal and any others that Suzanne manages to place will only be open at certain times during the day. And just for ninety seconds. If we miss it, we'd have to wait until the next day.

"You all have been given a tracker that will vibrate when you are near a portal. If you are in trouble, and if there is nothing you can do, then use it to return home. Otherwise, note where the portal is in case we need it later. We plan to stay together and go back together, but we don't know what we'll find."

We all nodded. Each of our trackers were hidden in different places on our bodies. But they were all placed so that they were as unobtrusive as possible. Mine was under the band of my bracelet.

Before we left, Leif had set a binding spell on my bracelet so it couldn't be lost or taken away from me. I assumed he had done that for everyone, and even I didn't know where each tracker was on each person. The only ones without trackers were the Priscillas. So whomever they were traveling with was responsible for their returning safely.

Niko shook his head at us. "Now see there? You all unconsciously checked to make sure your tracker was in place. Never do that again. It's an old pickpocketing trick used in the Earth Realm.

"Someone would announce there were pickpockets in the

area and everyone would check to make sure they still had their purses or wallets. The watching thieves then knew precisely where their valuables were.

"We can't make those kinds of mistakes."

After looking at all of us to make sure we had all heard him he added, "Now let's find the best place to settle in, and we'll talk more later."

Before we left our time, we had set up some basic plans. The first thing we were supposed to do was get acclimated to our new place in time. Professor Link had suggested that traveling back in time might be similar to traveling to different time zones in the Earth dimension, and resting and getting used to our surroundings would be a good thing. We had all resisted the idea at first, but eventually agreed that he was right.

Once we rested, we needed to explore Erda as it was then. What was different, what was the same? Not knowing could be dangerous.

Pita and Teddy wanted to find the local Ginete and Whistle Pigs and enlist them in helping the same way they did in the future. The idea that they learned how to do the things they knew how to do because we were here in the past flitted through my mind, and I shut it down immediately before I went crazy. Still, it was possible, right?

Ruta also wanted to spend time with the trees. He wanted to move through them and collect information. The Priscillas were itching to find some insect or animal friends and hear what they had to say.

We were all to remain as invisible as possible except when contacting the people we hoped would be our allies. There had been a debate as to if we would tell anyone that we were from the future or keep it to ourselves. The decision was made not to.

First, would they even believe us, and second, telling them

might once again affect something in the future so it wouldn't be the same when we returned.

But all that exploring wasn't going to happen this first day. Instead, we explored where the portal had placed us, being careful to leave as small a trace as possible. Niko and Aki had told us that there were lookouts stationed many miles out from the village, and we didn't want to run into any of them. So as much as Niko and Aki wished to see their home, they had to control that desire.

Professor Link had mapped some caves to the north of the village. If they were empty, they would be the perfect place for us to stay for a few days while exploring the area. We found one of the caves right before the sun went down.

Zeid and Niko went in first. Zeid threw an invisibility cloak over them and Niko used a light that he found in his backpack. Teddy said the beam would not be visible to anyone looking at it but would light up the surroundings for them.

After what felt like years, they returned, saying the cave was empty and looked as if it had been vacant for a long time. Everyone seemed as relieved as me. I was exhausted. The adrenalin rush of preparing to travel through the portal and then being back in time had worn off, and now all I wanted to do was sleep.

Within minutes I was sound asleep inside the sleeping bag that was attached to my backpack. I think I managed to whisper "Thank you, Teddy and Pita," before I fell asleep, but it might have been in my dreams.

Twenty-One

It took me a few minutes to figure out where I was. Nothing was familiar. The light was different. There was a dry smell in the air like old rocks and dirt. I wondered if I was dreaming and squirmed around in my sleeping bag trying to wake up.

"Stop it!" Pris yelled and bopped me on the nose.

"I thought I was dreaming," I said, holding my nose. "Was that necessary?"

When La and Cil stuck their heads out of the sleeping bag, I realized that they had all been sleeping inside of it with me.

My wiggling around had woken them up, and they were cranky. Keeping just my head outside the bag, I glanced around at where we were. The cave looked as if it was filled with mummies, everyone else still snuggling inside their bags. Maybe no one else felt like getting up and facing the day any more than I did.

Except for Aki and Niko, who were talking quietly in the back of the cave. As hard as I tried to hear them, I couldn't. Niko glanced over at me with one of his scary looks, and I slithered back into my bag taking the Priscillas with me. We must have fallen back asleep because the next thing I knew Zeid was shaking me telling me to get my lazy bones up.

After the sleeping bags were rolled and hooked back on our backpacks, we gathered around the fire that Zeid had started. I knew that there wouldn't be a fire if they thought there was a current danger of Abbadon's Raiders.

Which meant someone had already been out exploring, and others had stayed awake while I slept. The realization that I had been only thinking of myself fell over me like a blanket, smothering any sense of wonder about where we were that I might have otherwise felt.

"Stop it," Aki said.

Leave it to Aki to be in my mind. I could have left it alone, but instead, I said, "Stop what?" Even to my own ears, I sounded like a petulant teenager.

"And don't start doing the sorry thing, either," Aki said. "It was fine. We had it planned out who was doing what last night, and it will be your turn soon."

There wasn't anything to say, although I still wanted to either be mad at myself or feel sorry for myself. I squashed the temptation to be distracted and turned my attention back to the group huddled around the fire.

"This cave will remain our home base for the time being," Niko said. "Ruta reported back that the trees have not seen the Raiders yet.

"The trees were only vaguely aware of what Abbadon is doing. I understand that in the end, Ruta had to tell them who he is and where he is from. Trees understand time better than we do so they weren't as surprised or confused as some other beings might be with the idea that we are from the future.

"The trees have agreed to work with Ruta to pass the message to all the trees. For now just the trees. We don't want to broadcast to Abbadon that we are here. The trees know how to be silent and keep information to themselves. From now on they are our prime sentinels. They will pass information through their network of roots which covers all of the Kingdom.

"They will report directly to Ruta what they find, and in that way we might be able to stay out of sight of Abbadon's forces while we build alliances with the beings that live here."

Looking around the room, Niko added, "We can't think that we can march up to Abbadon's Castle and capture him. Even as good as all of you are, it can't be done. We've seen the kinds of minions and evil things Abbadon knows how to produce. Some of them may already be here. I don't think any of us want to run into any version of the Shrieks or Deadsweep."

A shudder ran through me, and I felt sick. It hadn't occurred to me that these things would exist now.

Niko was still talking. "Even without those kinds of things, Abbadon is not alone. At this point in history, Abbadon is not working by himself. He has people and beings that work with and for him. Some of them because they are afraid not to, and others because they believe in his mission."

"How could they believe in his mission?" I asked. "He wants to destroy all living things which would include them, and their families at some point."

"Obviously that is not the mission that he is telling them about. We need to find out what he is teaching and promising. Which means we will have to become part of the communities that already exist here.

"But first we have decided to rescue our mother."

"But not rescue our younger selves," Aki added.

"It's a good choice," Garth said as the rest of us sat in stunned silence.

Garth and Anne had been quiet since the moment we arrived. Actually, they had always been quiet, taking in what people were saying but not adding much to the conversation.

They were the most experienced dimension travelers in the Kingdom, and also the ones that had helped build the time-portal with Suzanne. But they had never shared what they thought about our team's planning.

All eyes swiveled to Garth. He and Anne looked as if they had lived in caves all their lives. Maybe no matter where they were they looked as if they were at home. It was probably a talent that they needed. They both wore their red hair short. I thought that perhaps it was easier to take care of when doing the kind of traveling that they did, and then I realized it might be something else.

It made it easier to disguise Anne as a man. Instead of a brother and sister team, it would be two brothers. It had never occurred to me that traveling as a woman would be more dangerous. Probably because I always had a team with me.

Anne looked over at me and smiled. I smiled back at her. It had finally dawned on me that she and I could be friends. Like real friends. Like sister friends. This time when she smiled at me her eyes lit up. Of course, she knew what I was thinking. I held up my pinky finger, and she did the same. It was a pinky promise.

As discreet as we were trying to be, Ruta had seen. I thought that he might be mad at me for being distracted, but instead, he gave me one of his tiny smiles that only those that knew him well understood to be a smile. Otherwise, it looked more like a twitch. Gratitude for Ruta swelled up inside of me threatening to spill over.

Then Pris pulled my hair, Beru wasn't there to pinch my leg, and I turned back to listen to what Garth had to say.

Twenty-Two

Garth had remained silent after his statement, and we all waited for him to continue. Garth looked a little surprised that he had spoken up, but he didn't look any less sure of what he said.

"Glad you think so, Garth," Niko said, "But perhaps you would like to explain why you think this is a good idea."

Garth paused before continuing. "To clarify, I am still wondering about rescuing your mother, but I definitely agree that you two should not stop what is going to happen to your child self. In fact, Anne and I think that no one should rescue anyone who we know is still alive in the future."

"What if they're dead in the future?" Ruta asked. Everyone knew why Ruta had stepped outside of his usual reluctance to say anything in a meeting. His village had been destroyed. His mother had died. My breath caught in my throat. He was asking for me, too.

Garth took a deep breath and looked as if he wanted to sink into the floor. "It's possible that it also would be too dangerous for the future."

Looking at both Ruta and me he added, "Are either of you two more than you might have been if your mothers had lived?

If your village had not been destroyed, Ruta, would you be here with this team? Would you have found Beru?"

The truth of what he said hit me like a sledgehammer. It was true. I wouldn't be wearing my mother's bracelet. I probably wouldn't have met Ruta if his village was still there.

"Wait," I said. "If we stop Abbadon in this time frame aren't we already rescuing all these people that we want to rescue? If Abbadon didn't have time to destroy Ruta's village, won't our mothers be there when we get back?"

"Yes, but you might not be there. We might not be there. Some, or all of us, might not make it back. Or we might be totally different people. However, we would have saved the Kingdom. Isn't that what we signed up for? To save the Kingdom?"

Seeing my face, Garth added more gently, "I know that the ramifications of what we are doing are not something we will know until it's all over. But you did know the possibilities, didn't you? And even if you didn't, and now you do, would you choose anything different? Wouldn't you still be here?"

Garth looked around the cave and added, "Wouldn't we all still be here? Isn't that what we came for? Perhaps we will be stuck back here. Maybe if we get to step through the time-portal, we don't come out the other side because we don't exist in the future anymore after what we have done.

"Maybe all of you didn't fully realize what could happen until now. But even so, wouldn't you all still be here?"

No one moved. The only sound was the fire crackling in front of us.

It was Zeid who broke the silence. "Yes, I would still choose to be here. And you're right. Until you said all of that sitting here in this cave back in time, I hadn't fully realized what could happen.

"However, I think that you and Anne fully understood, and yet you came with us. You could have just helped set up the time-portals with Suzanne, and then taught us what we needed to know and stayed behind. Why did you two come even though you knew the risks better than the rest of us?"

Garth looked at Anne and nodded for her to answer.

"Because we may have set this in motion, and now we have to stop it."

****

If I thought that the cave had been silent before, I was wrong. This time I swear even the fire stopped making a sound. All the air whooshed out of the cave and then roared back in. Really roared. Like Earl, or Coro. And then Earl was there. Standing at the entrance, looking just as we had left him.

Stunned we all stared. What was going on? If Earl could travel back in time why didn't he tell us that? The idea that Anne and Garth had caused Abbadon to be a monster took second place in the order of questions that needed to be answered.

Earl didn't stay. Assuming that was Earl. We blinked, and he was gone, but not before we all heard the word, "No."

Since Professor Link wasn't there to say anything I used his line, "Well, that was interesting…" and we all laughed again. Not quite as freely as the first time. But it was enough to get us all talking.

It was Teddy who asked the question. "Was that Earl? Why was he here? What did he mean, when he said, 'no?'"

We all looked at each other as if one of us would know the answer, and we all ended up back at Anne.

I wouldn't have thought that her face could get any whiter, and yet there she was looking like a frozen porcelain doll. Garth didn't look much better.

Finally, Anne spoke. "I guess Earl didn't like what I said."

"Well, that was pretty obvious. The not liking it part," I responded trying not to sound as snarky as I felt. After all, I had just made a pinky promise with Anne to be friends.

"'No' is pretty easy to understand. But how could that be Earl and why would he be so upset about what you said? Shouldn't we all be upset that you might have started all these problems? Wait, that's what Earl didn't want us to believe right? He came back here to keep us from blaming you. I don't get it …" I said finally running out of steam.

Taking a deep breath, I added, "Seriously, I don't get it. And I doubt anyone else does either. I'll be quiet now and let you explain. You can, can't you?" My voice had taken on a decidedly whiny tone.

Niko spoke instead. "Let's clarify what we need to know. This all started because you said you agreed with us not to rescue ourselves as children. And then not to rescue anyone that we know is still alive, or even dead, in the future."

Garth nodded, and Niko continued, "What about our mother? We assume she died because we never saw her again. But perhaps she survived it. Do you think it would be okay to rescue her if it is possible?"

"Next, was that Earl? If no, who was it? If yes, how did he do that and why? And finally, and definitely not last, what do you mean when you said you two might have caused it? Start wherever you want to begin. Oh, and one more thing. Why would we listen to you?"

"Other than the fact that Earl might have shown up to tell us about them?" I said.

Niko nodded. "Point taken. Okay, go. One of you talk. Like now."

Twenty-Three

Anne started to answer, but then Pita raised his hand. Pita raising his hand was so weird, it stopped us all in our tracks.

"I think I can answer a few of these questions," Pita said. "In fact, I may be the only one who can, so may I speak?"

Niko shook his head as if trying to clear it, but then gestured at Pita to continue. I thought back to when I had first seen the Ginete.

Pita and his four brothers had met us all at the tavern in Dalry. At the time, their large heads and huge golden eyes made me think they looked like a cross between a dwarf and a lighthouse. Later, Pita and his brothers, in fact, all the Ginete had been instrumental in stopping Abbadon's last few monsters.

After I met them, I became curious about why the village seemed to respect the brothers and at the same time be a little afraid of them. I had never seen anything that would make me fearful of the Ginete. But on the other hand, I had no idea what their history was with the town.

Other than being a cousin of the Whistle Pigs, I knew very little about the Ginete. It wasn't totally my fault. Pita and his brothers were friendly, but also very private.

Pita and his brothers had been the ones who had prepared

the remembering ceremony for me before we went on our first mission together. It made sense that they could run a tradition like that only if they knew much more about the workings of Erda than met the eyes.

When Teddy put his hand on Pita's shoulder, I realized that it was possible that he knew what Pita was going to say. But it could have just been his way of telling him that no matter what he would be there for him. If I had been sitting close enough to Pita, I would have done the same thing.

Aki got up and came back with more wood for the fire. Pita waited for her to return and then spoke. "I know why Anne and Garth are worried that they may have precipitated the beginnings of Abbadon's reign of terror. I also know why the vision of Earl showed up.

"My brothers and I were not alive in this time-period. But the story was carefully told to us, so when the right moment arrived, we would be able to repeat it. I didn't know this was that time until just a few minutes ago, or I would have spoken up sooner."

"What do you mean the vision of Earl?" Aki asked. "Are you saying that wasn't, Earl?"

"Yes and no, or more accurately no and yes," Pita answered. When Ruta snorted, Pita added, "I am not trying to be dense or confusing. It's part of the story."

"Zut," Niko said. "Then tell the ziffering story."

Niko swearing was unusual. He was usually unflappable. But we all understood.

Pita held up his hand, closed his eyes halfway so we could only see the bottom of his eyes. I recognized that look. It was one where he was trying to think.

"Okay. The story begins when the scenario Anne and Garth are referring to happened. The Earl from this time-period knew that one day they would blame themselves. So he programmed a holograph that would show up the minute one of them said what Anne said.

"I had heard that Earl would only say the word 'no.' The reason is precisely what you think it would be. He didn't want them to take the blame or responsibility for Abbadon's evil."

"So it was your people that were there?" Anne whispered. "They saw what happened, and then told the story so people wouldn't forget? And Earl programmed that hologram just for us?"

Pita nodded, and Anne burst out into tears, covering her face and leaning forward until all we could see was the top of her head. Garth put his arm around his sister to comfort her, but we could see him fighting off his own tears.

In a way, I was delighted to learn that it wasn't actually Earl standing in the doorway of the cave because then I would have been a teeny, tiny, bit angry that he hadn't told us he could travel in time. On the other hand, he hadn't told us a lot of things. That thought made me snicker to myself. Who had?

It felt as if every time I turned around someone else was telling us something else that we hadn't known before. I wondered what other secrets still hadn't been revealed.

The Priscillas had been sitting on my lap while all of this was going on. Normally, they would have been flitting from person to person, trying to get close to the action. And if not that, they would be trying to liven things up. I glanced down at them, and La raised her head to look at me.

I leaned over and whispered to them. "What's going on? Are you three okay?"

All three of them shook their heads, no. "Do you feel sick?"

"No," La whispered so that only I could hear. "Not in the way you mean. But yes in another way."

This time all three Priscillas nodded yes. "Is this another secret? Something you haven't told before?"

Another yes nod from all of them and then all three buried their faces in my lap and started to cry.

I looked up to see Anne looking at me.

"It's not their fault. We asked the Priscillas not to tell."

"Not tell what?"

"The story of what happened."

This time it was my turn for my face to turn white, but then I started to feel a surge of anger that scared me. I knew what could happen if I didn't control it. Lightning balls were not going to be a good thing inside a cave.

"When did you make them promise?" I asked through clenched teeth at my new best friend who was rapidly becoming a past friend.

"Back then, when it happened," Anne answered.

Twenty-Four

If the Priscillas had not been on my lap, I would have stood up and shot those lightning bolts, cave or no cave. Instead, I said in the calmest voice I could manage, "Start talking. And this better be good, or I'm voting that we leave you behind."

Niko gave me a look that scared the ziffer out of me before saying. "I don't care how angry you are Miss Kara Beth, we never, ever, leave anyone behind. Including you in case you are in a fit of temper."

Turning from me, he addressed Garth and Anne, "On the other hand, you two have a lot of explaining to do. And before we go out into this world and start interacting with it, you better tell us the whole story, and don't leave anything out."

Aki stood. "I agree. However, I think it would be wise to check our surroundings to be sure that we are still safe, and perhaps gather more wood for the fire, and eat something before we begin."

Then she turned to Garth and Anne and added, "But you two are staying here. I would like Kara to stay with you, but at the moment she isn't your best friend, and everyone else has something to do, so we are going to have to trust that you will stay put."

After receiving a nod from the two of them, Aki assigned everyone else something to do, and then she dissolved away. I assumed she needed some time to herself.

Ruta went to check with the trees. Pita and Teddy were still looking for signs of other Ginete and Whistle Pigs. Zeid and Niko said they were going to check the area for any changes that might have happened overnight and would bring some firewood back with them.

That left the Priscillas and me with nothing to do, but Aki was right. I didn't want to sit in the cave with Garth and Anne by myself. Instead, the four of us sat outside under a huge oak tree, and I thought about what would happen to this land unless we stopped Abbadon. In our time, all of this land was barren and shattered. What could have ever caused something like this to happen, and what did the Priscillas have to do with it?

I didn't ask them. They had promised not to tell, and as fierce and sometimes feisty as the Priscillas are, I knew they would never break a promise, and I would not ask it of them. We ate a little food that Beru had packed for us and waited in silence for the return of the team.

They weren't long. Niko and Zeid were the first. Then Pita and Teddy and Ruta. Aki appeared right after that and ushered us all inside.

Once we were all seated, and everyone reported that all was calm on the outside, Niko motioned for Anne and Garth to begin. If anyone had found anything outside, it appeared they were going to wait until this was settled before sharing it.

However, before Anne could begin, Pris flew off my shoulder and hovered in front of Anne and Garth. She was joined by Cil and La.

Once again, surprisingly it was Cil who spoke. "We are worried that because of us you won't fairly hear what happened.

So you need to know, that they asked us not to tell for our safety. Not theirs."

La looked at her sisters who both nodded and then settled down in Anne's lap instead of mine. All three smiled at me, and I smiled back. They were supporting Anne, and I loved them for it.

Their announcement removed all the bitterness from the room. They were right. We weren't going to hear the story fairly.

"Thank you," Niko said to the Priscillas. "I do believe that we are ready to listen now, Anne."

Anne closed her eyes for a moment, sighed, smiled down at the Priscillas in her lap and said, "I wish I could start this story with the words Once-Upon-A-Time as if it hadn't happened. But it did.

"Garth and I are even older than we told you before. We have been traveling between dimensions for hundreds and hundreds of years. Sometimes we stay for a while if it is a place that we can fit in without being seen as outsiders. Other times we have to leave almost immediately because nothing is the same as here, or it is too dangerous.

"We learned the skill from our parents, who were part of a small group of people in Erda who are also dimension travelers. Our job has been to learn and share what we learn when the information is needed. In many ways, we are living historians. Not just of Erda but of many other dimensions that exist on the planet we call Gaia. It's a dying art, though. There are only a few of us left. Either the others find a dimension that they are happier in and stay there, or something happens to them, and they never return.

"As much as we enjoy this work, it is often dangerous, and sometimes things go wrong. And in one of our travels, something went terribly wrong.

"At first we didn't know anything was wrong. We stepped through the portal and found a beautiful world. It looked just like Erda, which was surprising in a way, but it made us happy. We had talked about finding another dimension that we could stay in if we got tired of Erda, or if something went awry, and this looked like one we could keep in mind.

"We spent a few weeks exploring. We didn't meet anyone at first. In fact, we tried not to. It was what we usually do when we travel.

"We take time to soak in the feel of the world, get to know how nature works there, and once we feel as if we are part of the dimension we will search out whoever lives there. We think it's important to not look like a stranger.

"Besides, the dimension we thought we had traveled to was so beautiful we wanted to enjoy it as much as possible before getting to know the people, or beings, the dimension belonged to.

"Finally, we made our way towards a village. We watched from a distance and were struck again by how much the people looked like the people of Erda, except it was a little off. We just couldn't put our finger on it. When we felt we were ready, we walked into the village.

"It only took us a few minutes to discover that we had made a huge mistake. We had not gone into another dimension the way we had planned. Something had gone wrong within the portal. We had gone back in time."

Twenty-Five

Anne held up her hand as we all started to talk. "I know you all have questions, but if you would let me tell the story, I think it will answer most of them. I'll make it as brief as possible.

"We don't know how it happened. And much later when we managed to get back to our own time, we found the tiny mistake that had been made, and it never was made again. But it did help us design the portal we used to get here, so I suppose some good has come out of it.

"On the other hand, if it wouldn't have occurred, perhaps none of what Abbadon has done would have happened, and we wouldn't have to be here now putting all of you in danger."

'We don't know that," Garth interjected. I could tell he was having trouble letting Anne tell the story.

"I think you have to look at what Earl did just to make sure you didn't try to blame us, and especially yourself for what happened. We didn't make the mistake that brought us back here, and it wasn't your fault that Abbadon fell in love with you."

We all gasped, Anne closed her eyes and sagged back against the wall. Garth looked around the room at all of us staring at the two of them.

"I suppose I shouldn't have just blurted it out that way, but if you want the short version of the story, I think I am the one to tell you. Anne is still going to try to take responsibility for what happened, and I can't let her. I don't think our friends the Priscillas plan to let her either." They looked up at him and nodded.

"So we found out that we were in the past. Now we had a problem. We didn't know if we got into the portal if it would take us back to the time we came from or if we would end up somewhere else.

"Yes, if we would have been brave enough, we probably would have marched right back to the portal and stepped in. But we weren't. On the other hand, we were the first people we had ever heard of that had gone back in time. We couldn't help wondering what we would discover that could help the future if we made it back home.

"We're basically historians and collectors of information. Here we were in a world we never expected to find ourselves in. So combining that with our curiosity and our fear that we might not make it back to the future, we decided to stay a while.

"At the time, we didn't know about affecting the future, but because of our dimension traveling, we knew it was always best to keep a low profile.

"To fit in, we made up an almost true story. We were traveling historians. We just left out the part that we were from the future. The village was kind to us, and we loved meeting the people. We helped out in their stores, and in the fields, and in return they fed and housed us. It was always our intention to return home, but we got comfortable. We almost forgot that we didn't belong there.

"Both of us thought about staying. I met a girl that I liked, and that increased the temptation to settle in that time period.

"What we hadn't realized was that Abbadon's Castle was not that far from the village of King's Watch, although I suppose the name gave it away. At the time, he wasn't well known, but he also wasn't the monster that we know him to be today.

"The people looked up to him because he was the King. Once a year he held a ball at the Castle that everyone could attend. I think it was more a publicity thing than an act of kindness, but it did make the people think well of him.

"It was a huge event for the village. All the girls loved going. It was a chance to dress up. Of course, the women of King's Watch told Anne she had to go. It didn't take much persuading."

Garth looked over at his sister and smiled at her. "Anne is beautiful, but in some ways, she hides it now. She didn't then. Anne looked stunning in the gown one of the girls in town loaned to her. She had long hair then, and it was bound up into some complicated hairstyle.

"Anyway, you can guess what happened. Anne went to the ball. Abbadon saw her, and the story goes that he immediately fell in love with her.

"Since I had already thought about staying, we both agreed that there was no harm in seeing the King. After all, that would make her a Queen if their relationship progressed that far."

Anne put a hand on her brother to stop, and she took over.

"Abbadon was handsome, and although a little full of himself, he was generous and kind to me, and when he noticed the people of the village, he was kind to them, too. I was caught up in the glamour of being the King's favorite.

"I met the Priscillas a few months later. At the time they were living in the forest and would come into town once in a while. Mostly to play practical jokes on people and have a little fun. No one minded. Everyone loved them. Just as they do now."

The Priscillas giggled and looked down as Anne continued.

"After I got to know them, they stayed with me more often. It was because of them that I started asking myself if what I was doing was the right thing. Did I really want to stay back in time? I missed my friends.

"I knew I would miss the people that I met in the village, but the urge to try to go home became greater than my fear about stepping into the portal.

"Garth and I talked and talked about it. Finally, we decided to leave. He told his girlfriend that it was time for us to move on. We were traveling historians after all. We had managed to keep the secret that we were from the future from everyone, except for the Priscillas who figured it out. Once they did, they were insistent that we return to the future. I think they also knew Abbadon better than I did.

"Then it was my turn to tell Abbadon. We went for a walk as we often did. Unknown to me, thankfully the Priscillas came with me. I think they were worried. For a good reason, it turned out. I told Abbadon how much I cared about him, but it was time for my brother and me to return home.

"Only then did I see the side of him that has grown into the monster we know today. He was furious. The more I tried to explain how much I cared about him and was sorry to leave, the angrier he got. He hit me, and I fell."

Anne paused and took a drink of water. I looked over at Pita and realized he knew this story.

Anne looked over at Pita too as she continued. "It was two Ginete that saved me. I didn't know they were your family, Pita, or I would have thanked you long ago.

"They heard me screaming and came running. The Priscillas were doing their best to fight Abbadon off of me, but brave as they were it wasn't enough.

"I don't know how the Ginete got us away from him, but they did. As we ran, we could hear Abbadon yelling that he would punish everyone I loved from now until forever.

"The Ginete found my brother, took care of us until I was better, and then Garth and I returned to the portal, which happily brought us back to our own time.

"Since then Abbadon has been keeping his promise. Not just punishing me, but all of Erda."

Twenty-Six

I couldn't believe it. I was so furious that I stood up and yelled, "Abbadon became a monster because you broke his heart?"

Zeid reached up and pulled me back down beside him. Anne burst into tears.

"I'm sorry Anne, that wasn't meant for you. You didn't do anything wrong. People break up every day and move on. They don't beat on the person they claimed to love or destroy things. Abbadon is a stalker, serial killer, psycho with extraordinary powers. He is magic gone wrong, and your story made me even more grateful for being here so we can stop him now."

Everyone murmured in agreement, and Anne whispered, "Thank you."

"I have a question," Zeid said, "Why didn't we go back to that time where you were, and take care of him when he was still not as powerful as he is now?"

It was Pita who answered Zeid. "We did. We are here before Anne breaks his heart. We are here before Niko and Aki are captured. And we are here before Abbadon destroys villages. But that doesn't matter. The trigger to Abbadon's madness happened years before Anne met him. He was destroying things long before they got here. That's another reason why Abbadon's destruction of the planet isn't Anne or Garth's fault."

Turning to Garth and Anne, Niko asked, "Is that true? We are here before you got here the first time?"

When they nodded affirmatively, Niko turned to Pita, "And how did you know this?"

"It's in the story my family has told. They saw us when we arrived from the future. It's confusing and hard to explain, but they saw us after they rescued Anne. They remembered a past that would become the future." Pita shrugged and added, "It's a gift that my people have."

I was beginning to understand why the people of Dalry both admired the Ginete and feared them a little too. "So your people see timelines and remember them? In a way, I understand that. It would be like reading a book about something that happened that didn't happen yet. Wait, I'm not sure that makes sense when I put it into words, but it makes a little bit of sense when I feel it inside."

Pita smiled at me and said, "Not bad. I am not sure how to explain it better. I should tell you though that this kind of memory isn't a constant. My brothers and I do not hold multiple timelines in our head, nor for the most part, remember them. But when it's important, the story gets passed down, or a memory surfaces, as in this case because it is so important."

Teddy grunted and stood up, taking up as much space as he could. "Talk, talk, talk. Tired of talking."

We all stared at him, "Okay, so I guess I need to know a few more things before we go gallivanting all over the countryside. But could we do it later? The only thing I want to know right now is if we are going to run into the Anne and Garth from the future, and if we do, how will we know which one it is, and what should we do?"

Anne laughed. It was the first time I had ever heard her laugh, but I understood why she did. Teddy made everything better, just by being Teddy. I wouldn't be surprised if he started giving her unique names too.

"Yes, you might. This is the area we stayed in, but not in this cave. However, at this time we are living in the village of King's Watch. But if for some reason you see us you'll know which one of us it is. First off, I had hair. A lot of hair. And we wore very different clothes this time, on purpose. You won't have any trouble telling us apart."

"Well, then Pita and I are off. Pita says he knows where to find the Ginete." Teddy paused and looked at his friend. "Oh, now I know why you wanted to wait. You wanted me to know that I was meeting your family, from the past."

Teddy grabbed Pita and hugged him. It was an odd sight. A bear-like being was embracing a squat, big-eyed, big-headed creature. Teddy slapped Pita on the back, which actually made Pita smile, and said, "Okay, mate, let's go meet the past."

As they sauntered out of the cave together, I looked at Zeid and said, "Mate?" Everyone laughed including Teddy who overheard me. He stuck his head back into the cave and said, "Righty-oh! See you all back here around dinner."

The Priscillas, taking a cue from Teddy and Pita, were also heading out of the cave. They didn't bother to say where they were going.

I used to worry about them when they did that and then tried to stop them from heading off without telling me where they were going.

But Pris had made it abundantly clear that they didn't like it when I tried to control them, even if it was out of love. This time I was happy to see them go. That meant they had a plan. We would all learn about it when it was the right time, just as it was the right time for them to fly out of the woods and help Anne.

Is that where they were going? To help Anne again? The other Anne? It was hard for me to grasp that the Priscillas that had been with me since childhood had been with Anne hundreds of years before that. They chose us both—another reason for me to get to know Anne better.

I was so busy thinking about the Priscillas and Anne that I didn't see Ruta leave. He had remained silent the whole time we were talking about the past. Usually, that meant he knew something and wasn't sharing it. But like the Priscillas, he would tell us when it was time.

Niko turned to the rest of us, "Aki, Garth, and I are going to check on our former home, Willowdale. Zeid, you, Anne, and Kara will check on King's Watch. For Zut's sake, stay out of sight and just observe what is happening there. Don't do anything!

"I'll cloak the cave so no one will see it while we are gone. Be careful. We still don't know the whole story of what happened back here."

"No kidding," I mumbled under my breath. And then I realized that Anne was going with us. I would drag more information out of her. Niko caught my eye as we left the cave together, and I realized that was precisely what he wanted me to do.

I winked, he winked back, and we were off in different directions, but with the same goal in mind.

Twenty-Seven

Since Anne knew the way, we let her lead us towards King's Watch where her past self now lived. We walked in silence, all of us busy with our thoughts. It didn't take long before thinking took second place to what we were seeing.

The forest was full of life, and as we kept our energy withdrawn, the birds and animals had no trouble revealing themselves to us. We saw everything from a red fox to a woodcock who treated us to his dance. We did our best not to laugh. His dance was so silly, but we didn't want to hurt his feelings.

My favorite were the chickadees that followed us as we walked, chattering to themselves about the strangers in their woods. However, social creatures that they are, within minutes the chickadees were flying down in front of us to check us out and say hello.

Hawks, squirrels, deer, all were present. As long as we kept our energy field as invisible as possible, they showed no fear, just curiosity. Although there were more evergreens than in our eastern forests, it was almost like being in our woods back home and in our time.

After a while the trees got into the act, lifting their

branches to let us pass, or opening a view for us to see. When they revealed one particularly stunning view of the distant mountains, we took a moment to rest and admire the beauty of where we were.

Of course, rocks were right where we needed them to be for us to have a place to sit. It was so lovely I could have stayed there forever, but the knowledge that in our time all of this beauty would be shattered and destroyed reminded me that we had a job to do.

Not long after that, we found the place where Anne and Garth had observed King's Watch before entering it. We settled in to do the same thing. I could tell Anne was upset, which made perfect sense, but I thought maybe talking about it would help. Besides, I was supposed to gather information from her. We were hidden from view, and there was no one else to hear us, so I spoke up.

"How hard is this for you?"

Anne sighed. "I knew this would be hard—all of it. We knew we would have to tell you all the truth about what happened. I hoped it wouldn't make everyone hate me."

She smiled at me when I shook my head no at her.

"You have no idea how much it means to my brother and me that you all understood. It's been painful keeping it a secret for all these years and seeing the destruction that Abbadon is doing and thinking perhaps it was my fault. Yes, I do have my hair short now so that I won't always be seen as a woman. I know you figured that out. It's just too painful.

"We escaped the pain as much as possible when we traveled to other dimensions. Some were more messed up than this one, and in some there wasn't much life there yet. But Earth and Erda were manipulated, and that I think has been both a blessing and a curse."

Zeid and I looked at her in shock. "Are you talking about Aki's Once-Upon-A-Time story about the two bored brothers in the spaceship?"

"Do you still think that was a fairy tale because of the way she told it?"

"I hoped it was," I answered.

"No," Anne said, shaking her head. "Sadly, it's true. In Earth and Erda it's the Cain and Abel story. In the Earth dimension, the killing happens almost immediately and from then on Earth has struggled with war and misunderstandings. People against people. People against nature. People who have lost their awareness of their true identity.

"In Erda, they separated Darius and Abbadon. They put them on opposite ends of the Continent. There was no need to interact. They both had everything that they wanted.

"Also, the brothers instilled in the beings of Erda a greater sense of the wonderment of magic, an appreciation for diversity, a knowledge that everything is alive and aware. They fostered respect, appreciation, and partnership with nature.

"You know how that went. Erda, at least in the Kingdom of Zerenity, has lived in peace and harmony for thousands of years. Then something happened, and Abbadon was no longer satisfied. No longer happy."

"What happened?" Zeid and I asked at the same time.

"That's what we don't know. Yes, I blamed myself for Abbadon's increased anger and destruction, but something happened before then. When we were here last time, we were not aware of it. The townspeople seemed to be happy. Everything was still beautiful. I had only the smallest feeling that all was not right with Abbadon when I was with him.

"Perhaps that's why I couldn't fall completely in love with him. Something was off. He was kind and caring, and yet distant. I know that I put it down to the fact that he was a King and perhaps he thought it gave him a right to be more self-important. It was only when he couldn't get what he wanted that he became violent, and revealed the monster that lived underneath that pretty exterior."

While Anne was talking something occurred to me. I should have thought of it before, but with so much going on I had missed it. Anne was a dimension traveler. She knew the Earth and Erda story.

Anne giggled and patted my hand. "Yes, we have been to the Earth dimension. And before you jump out of your skin with questions, I'll tell you that yes, we observed you as Hannah. You didn't think that your parents had only Suzanne checking on you, did you?"

I stared at her in amazement. "You knew me then? Did I know you?"

Anne didn't have time to answer because Zeid whispered and pointed down to the village of King's Watch and asked, "Is that you and Abbadon?"

Twenty-Eight

The three of us turned our eyes toward the town. In their infinite wisdom and creative abilities, the Whistle Pigs had given us all a pair of glasses that did multiple things. They helped us see in the dark, acted as sunglasses, and could be switched to be either a microscope or telescope. They had even made them stylish and fit each of us perfectly.

Anne and I switched to the telescope view and watched as a woman with long flowing red hair walked down the street holding the hand of a very handsome man. The same man that I had seen in the drawings of the man who had been living at the Castle.

Unconsciously I hissed at him. But even from a distance, I could see how Anne might have been attracted to him. Abbadon and Anne had turned to look at each other, holding hands as they stared in each other's face. If I could read lips, I might have been able to tell what they were saying.

When I glanced at Anne, tears were running down her face.

"He was telling me how beautiful I was, and how much he loved spending time with me. When he was with me, he didn't dress or act like a King. He was kind and attentive, with sad eyes. But even then I knew something was off because the townspeople were polite to him, but stayed away.

"You can see that there is no one close to us. They stayed inside or on the other side of the street. Once again, I thought it was because he was the King and they were being respectful. I was so young and naive."

We both waited for Anne to collect herself before Zeid asked, "How many days later did you tell him you were leaving. Can you remember?"

"Yes, it was three days from now. Garth and I woke with the same thought. We had to return home. And to answer your next question, no, I can't think of anything that happened that made that so evident. But maybe something did.

She turned to look at us and added, "Maybe it was someone from this team."

We all looked at each other wondering if that could be true. Zeid said what we all knew, "Whichever way it happened, it looks as if we have three days to stop him."

****

On the way back to the cave we were silent again. My thoughts were going around and around in circles. Was it possible that somehow our team from the past interacted with Anne and Garth while they were in the past? And if that was true, how did that happen, and who was it?

I knew there would be more questions that needed answers once we got back to the cave. However, I had a personal one, so I asked the question that had been lingering in the back of my mind driving me crazy. I was getting used to being Kara Beth. Princess Kara Beth. The young woman with magic skills, and a fiancé who had waited for me in Erda while I lived in the Earth Realm.

But the memory of Hannah, the young girl who had lived in Earth through two short life times, remained with me. I knew I could never return, but I did dream about Earth from time to time.

Professor Link had been right. Being an Earth child has helped me in Erda, when I let it. Besides the magic that I had remembered how to do, I had a little part of me that was wiser than I would ever have been if I had never traveled to another dimension.

People in the Earth Realm talk about how travel opens the mind to more possibilities and makes them a little bit wiser, if they are willing. Imagine what someone who has traveled to a multitude of dimensions must know. Anne might appear about the same age as me, but she knew things I would never understand.

And the one thing I had to know before we returned to the cave and the current problem was how she had known me in the Earth dimension.

Anne dropped back to walk beside me, and said, "Go ahead. Ask your questions."

I smiled at her, grateful for her ability to read my mind. I figured she already knew what I was going to ask, but for the sake of clarity and for Zeid who I knew was curious too, I asked it out loud.

"When I saw Suzanne in the Earth dimension she was never substantial. I know when she was living there she was appeared as a solid, person, like everyone else. But once she stopped living there, and began to travel between Earth and Erda, she was more like a translucent mist.

"Now that I know you have been to Earth, were you like a mist, or like a solid person who lived there? And did Garth come with you?"

Zeid had only heard some of my Earth story. I'm not sure why I haven't told him more, maybe because there was Johnny. Or perhaps because I knew I wouldn't be returning so what difference would it make. Either way, he knew very little about my time in the Earth dimension, so when Anne turned to me with a smile and answered me, he didn't understand why I had to stop and sit down.

"Say it again, please," I begged. "I need to hear it again."

Anne took a deep breath and said, "Garth and I were there as two people that you knew. We didn't look like this, but we were there watching over you. Yes, you knew us both. We both worked at the Diner and your coffee shop, Your Second Home.

"After you returned to Erda we left too. To the people of Doveland, we moved away.

"While we were in the Earth dimension, we continued to travel to Erda to report back to your parents. But then your Erda mother was killed, and Suzanne brought you home, so we left too."

I could barely take it in, but I had to table all of what that meant to me and deal with it later because we were back at the cave and Teddy and Pita were waiting with smiles on their faces.

Twenty-Nine

Pita looked so happy that I actually ran up to him and hugged him. He resisted, struggling a little, and then relaxed a tiny bit, so I knew he liked it in spite of himself.

"What happened? Did you find your family? You did, didn't you?" I would have kept on questioning him forever without waiting for a response if Teddy hadn't said, "Tulip Toes, let him answer!"

When Pita still didn't say anything, perhaps because he was still getting over the shock of me hugging him, Teddy told what happened.

"Not surprisingly, they were waiting for us. That storytelling tradition that the Ginete have sure is handy. Plus the ability to see multiple timelines without making themselves crazy. Well, that is quite astonishing. Anyway, we were walking towards the mountains because Pita said that given a choice, they prefer to live inside a mountain instead of under the ground. Well, I knew that already you see.

"But Pita and his brothers have been graciously staying in the tunnels in order to do their part in defeating Abbadon. I guess this is part of the story. They knew that was what they were supposed to do before they did it. Once Abbadon is stopped, they can go back to the mountains."

Teddy stopped and looked at Pita, and we could almost see his heart swell with love.

"Of course that will mean that I will have to come to visit. Anyway, a group of Ginete were waiting for us not far from here. They walked us into a clearing and dropped us down into the tunnels built there.

"Yes, I know what you are thinking. There are tunnels here too? The Whistle Pigs and Ginete work together in this time frame too. Isn't that amazing?"

I wanted to make the hurry-up-and-tell-me sign to Teddy but he was obviously enjoying his story so much I restrained myself.

"I met relatives of mine too! They aren't like the Ginete. I mean knowing the future and stuff, but the Ginete had told them all about me, so I got lots of hugs. It was fantastic. I can't wait to tell everyone about this when we get back."

By then Niko, Garth, and Aki had returned to the cave and were listening. Teddy hadn't seen them yet, having his back to them, so when Niko said, "Get on with it Teddy. What happened?" Teddy was startled. Then he laughed.

"Okay. Sorry. They used the same circles that we do to move from the tunnels to the surface. And the tunnels and rooms look very similar. Not exactly the same, I mean time has passed, and things have improved ..."

Catching Niko's eyes, he hurried on.

"Anyway, besides meeting past family, some of whom were expecting us, we found out that they had already prepared a place for us to stay if we need to, and built tunnels that lead directly under the Castle.

"Besides that, they gave us a little history into what Abbadon has been doing. It's going to be harder than we thought to stop him. He's been waiting for us. The same way the Ginete have been waiting for us. But obviously not for the same reasons."

"And you're still smiling?" I asked.

"Well, heck, Miss Worry Wart, why not? After all, we are here together. I met past family. We've done the impossible before. Why not now?"

I didn't much appreciate being called Miss Worry Wart. I liked Tulip Toes much better, but Teddy was right, up to a point. Maybe he didn't know we had only three days to stop Abbadon who knew we were coming. Then it struck me, and I turned to Teddy, "If he knows we're coming, does he know where we are?"

Suddenly Ruta was there. I swear he stepped out of the tree trunk. Then again, I shouldn't have been surprised. That's what he does. He travels by tree.

He was shaking his head. What did he mean by that? Did he hear the question? Did he have the answer?

Ruta continued to shake his head as he walked into the cave. We all followed him as if he was the Pied Piper. I guess we expected him to say something once we got inside, but instead, he just stood there. I remembered him taunting me when I first came through the portal. I was beginning to think that it was better than the stoic blank look he was giving us now.

"What do you have to tell us, Ruta?" Niko finally asked, as gently as he could.

It was as if Niko's question popped him out of some kind of state and Ruta plopped down on the ground. Not all that easy, and definitely not graceful, being built like a block of wood. It was the first time I realized that Ruta was like a penguin. They look silly out of the water, but in the water they are graceful and flowing. I thought that Ruta within the tree system was entirely different than when he wasn't. I wondered if it was hard for him.

When Ruta said, "Yes," I thought he was answering me,

but he was answering the question about Abbadon. "And no," he continued. "Somehow Abbadon knows that we are here, but no he doesn't know where we are. And he is not expecting us specifically. He only knows that someone from the future is coming to stop him."

"How could he know that? And what is he planning to do to keep us from coming after him? And since I am in the mode of asking questions," I began, ignoring the laughter from Zeid because I am always asking questions, "what exactly is he doing right now that we have to stop? And finally, and really, not all that small of a question, how were we going to do that anyway?"

It was Aki that answered me. "First we are rescuing our mother so that she is no longer in danger. After that, we let our child selves get captured and taken to the Castle. Except some of the Raiders will not be Abbadon's men. They will be Niko and Zeid."

"You are sending them into the Castle? Are you crazy? He will recognize them." I paused. "Oh, maybe not, he hasn't met them yet. At least the way Niko looks now. But then you will be yourself in two different timelines. What will that do to the future?"

"Nothing," Niko answered. "I remember meeting myself, but I didn't know it was me until we came back here and it clicked in."

I slapped my forehead and leaned against the cave wall. This was getting crazier and crazier. How were we ever going to keep all of this straight and not make a mistake with all these crossing timelines?

Thirty

The moon was hanging low in the sky, a big orange ball throwing strange shadows into the woods. An owl hooted nearby and a second one answered. When a third returned their call, I knew it was Ruta letting us know that he was in place. He was stationed high in the trees, watching.

If the Priscillas had returned, they would have been up there with him, but they hadn't. I couldn't let myself worry about them. They knew how to take care of themselves, and if they hadn't come back yet, it was for a good reason.

Our plan to rescue Niko and Aki's mother, and then plant Zeid and Niko in the Castle as spies, was simple in the telling. We had gone over it over and over again until we all knew the details and could have repeated them in our sleep. What worried me was there were so many variables, and as always I had questions.

What if Abbadon knew what we were planning? What if he was sending the Raiders to capture Niko and Aki as children because he knew we were there now and the raid was really to catch us? What if Aki and Niko's mother didn't recognize her grown-up daughter and wouldn't follow her into the woods where we would be waiting?

What if Abbadon knew that Niko was going to join the Raiders so that he could get into the Castle? What if he knew that Zeid would then join him?

For Niko to hide among the Raiders wasn't going to be hard. He could easily change himself to look like one of the men working for Abbadon. All he had to do was tell a good story, something I was sure he knew how to do. After all, he and Aki had fooled us all for a long time, why not Abbadon?

Getting Zeid into the Castle was another story. He couldn't change into someone or something else. Besides, he looked like a future King.

But Zeid could transport himself wherever he wanted to go. All he needed to know was where he was heading, and then a few minutes to reorient himself after he materialized again. It wasn't his favorite magical trick, but he could do it.

Niko would let Zeid know where he was. Zeid would transport there. They would liberate some Raider clothing, and then they would both be spies in Abbadon's Castle the same way that Abbadon had been a spy in ours. What could go wrong?

Every single detail of that plan could go wrong. But I couldn't let myself think that way. Zeid and I needed to finish this, go back to our timeline, and live our lives together.

We all had our roles to play in this plan, and we had spent some time deciding who was the right person for each job.

However, before we could even begin, we needed someone to monitor what everyone was doing, the same way that Professor Link did back in our time.

Teddy was the unanimous choice. When we all raised our hands for him, Teddy blushed so bright red that it was visible through all that fur. So now we had a Teddy channel open in our heads instead of a Link channel.

It wouldn't be quite the same. Teddy likes to keep things

light even when everything is going crazy, while Professor Link is more serious. But hearing each other all the time was a vital part of every plan, and was always our safety net.

Garth, Anne, and I lay on the ground hidden by branches of the nearest trees. We didn't put them there. The trees had bent over and moved to protect us. I could feel them tremble in anticipation of what was to come. Or perhaps it was me.

Niko was already on his way to join the Raiders. Ruta and his trees had found the invaders about a mile from the cave, so it was a short walk. He planned to stumble into their camp claiming a drunken stupor had made him miss their leaving. He would beg them to let him come along and not tell, because otherwise, Abbadon would kill him for missing their departure. We were all counting on Niko to pull that act off because without his being part of the raid in the morning, things could go very badly.

Aki would be walking into her village, but not looking like the Aki we know. She would look like her people. Her job was to get her mother to follow her into the woods where we would be waiting before the Raiders arrived.

Pita was going to be our guide to the entrance to the tunnels after Aki returned with her mother. For now, he was back with Teddy fiddling around with some ideas they said they had. Those two were always coming up with something new, and it was always something we needed. I said a prayer of gratitude for the two of them.

Before we left, I clung to Zeid. Very uncharacteristic of me, but this whole travel to another time thing had me feeling as if parts of me were missing. And now the most important person in my life was off to do something so dangerous I couldn't stop thinking of all the things that could go wrong.

Zeid kept assuring me that all would be well, but I was

terrified anyway. There were so many moving parts, and I couldn't stop thinking about what Niko and Aki had told us Abbadon was doing.

The raid that was happening in the morning was something Abbadon had been doing in villages all across his Kingdom for years. He had left the village near his Castle alone, at least for now, but Niko said that other communities across the Kingdom had been decimated.

Whoever his Raiders didn't kill were taken to his Castle and either put to work or used for experimentation. Niko and Aki hadn't said what kind and I didn't want to know. I just wanted to stop it from happening.

When the prisoners died, which they often did, their bodies were used for fuel to heat the Castle and the other buildings within Abbadon's Keep. Some of the buildings were like the one that we destroyed after killing Shatterskin. Manufacturing plants where people were hooked up to machines and had their essence drained out of their bodies.

I knew that hearing these horrible things that Abbadon was doing when she knew him, made Anne sick. As we lay there waiting for the morning, she told me that she kept asking herself how she didn't realize what Abbadon was. How could she have missed it? How could he have been using people and other beings as an energy supply for the machines he would use to destroy every living thing and still be that man with the sad eyes?

It was a question none of us could answer.

Thirty-One

"I'm here."

The three of us turned our heads towards the voice, but we couldn't see anything. I recognized the voice. It was Aki. But although we had our glasses on that allowed us to see into the night, I couldn't see anyone other than Anne and Garth.

And then I felt a hand on my back and another covering my mouth, which was a good thing, because I screamed.

"Shh, it's me."

I turned my head towards the voice, trying not to throw up from fear, and this time I could see Aki lying right beside me as if she had been there all along. She didn't look like herself. Or she did. Because she was no longer the Aki she made herself look like to fit in our world, but the Aki that would fit into her village. She looked like her true self.

"How did you get beside me without any of us knowing it?" I practically hissed at her. She had scared the ziffer out of me, and when I get scared, I get angry. Niko had told me that it was good that I got angry. He'd rather see anger then cowering and being a victim. He just wanted me to control that anger so that fireballs didn't erupt from my hands by mistake. I could feel the heat in my palms and willed it to disappear.

"I was making a point," Aki said. "You've seen me do that many times. Disappear and reappear. Have you taken that into account as you lie here? Or are you only using your five senses? Kara Beth, you've been practicing seeing 4D without the star. Keep doing it tonight. If you need to, you can use your star. But for zut's sake, don't think that you will hear Abbadon's minions coming the same way that you could hear the Shrieks or Shatterskin."

In all my worrying, I had never thought of that. I thought of Aki and her ability as unique and something only she could do. I had never asked if others could do the same. Aki must have felt the combination of terror and shame that I felt because she reached over and grabbed my hand and smiled.

"It's a lot to take in, Princess. But I know you are capable. The three of you will be fine. I will be back before dawn, with my mother. Stay safe."

Aki had never called me Princess before. She paused a moment before vanishing, and repeated it, "Princess."

What was she telling me? Aki never wasted words. In my mind's eye, I could still see her, staring at me as if she was pushing an idea into my head. I realized that none of us had asked her what her mother looked like. In my head I heard, "Like me, silly."

Silly Princess is more like it, I thought. Of course, they would look alike. Beautiful. Not the same beautiful that Aki had taken on to fit in at the Castle, but still beautiful.

Aki and her brother were both still tall. Aki was still thin, and Niko still built like a statue, but they were both a pale blue color that shimmered in the sun and faded into translucency in the night.

Both had white hair. Niko kept his short and Aki kept hers long, just as it was in her chameleon look. Both had hooded pale blue eyes, eyes that I had sometimes seen on Aki. Perhaps when she wasn't bothering to hide herself as much.

They were both much longer limbed then their chameleon shapes which made them both look even more like gazelles. Niko had reminded me of a gazelle when I first saw him, so that quality had also shown through their disguise. Their hands were the same as ours, except they had six fingers on each hand. I assumed they had six toes too.

I heard Teddy laugh. "Oh, the things you think about, Silly Princess."

I dropped my face into the ground. Zounds, I always forget to not think on the open channel. "And to answer your question," I heard Aki say, "No, we have seven toes, the better for running."

Still wanting to disappear, I kept silent for fear of saying something even more idiotic. A few moments passed in silence and then we heard Niko say, "I'm here."

For a moment I thought he meant right beside me the same way that Aki had been, but he added. "They bought the story. But something is off with these people. I'll be back with more information in a few minutes. Have to go meet the head Raider. Since I was late, they have to punish me somehow."

We all heard the intake of Aki's breath and Niko's assurance that it was worth it whatever it was. While we waited, Ruta hooted from the tree even though he could have just as easily talked to us in our heads, but I knew that being at the top of a tree pretending to be a bird was like being in seventh heaven to Ruta.

Since I hadn't heard Zeid respond, I started worrying again. I tried to restrain myself, but worry won out, and I said, "Zeid, are you okay?"

"Silly Princess," was his response.

I was beginning to worry that I had given myself a name I would never live down when we heard Niko whisper, "I'm back."

He didn't say anything else. He was letting us listen in to what was going on inside of the Raider's camp. Many people were talking, or it sounded more like arguing.

And then one voice said, "Stop," and everyone stopped talking.

Anne froze beside me. "I recognize that voice," she whispered. She looked at her brother, her eyes wide with fear.

"Who is it?" Teddy asked.

Garth answered, "It's Abbadon. He's with the Raiders."

Thirty-Two

Fear took over. So many questions and no answers.

Niko was in the Raider's camp with Abbadon. Why was Abbadon there? Did he know Niko? Did he know where we were?

I knew that I was not the only one having those questions fly around in their head. I wanted to stand up and run to the camp and kill Abbadon right then before he knew we were coming.

I could feel Anne shaking so hard I was worried she was having a seizure. Garth had his arm around her, but he too was afraid, his eyes wide as we looked at each other in panic.

"Silly Princess," Teddy said, calming us all down for the moment with humor. When no one answered him, he tried again, using Link's style of communication. "Stop it."

It was an unfortunate choice of words since it was the phrase that we had all just heard Abbadon utter, but at least it jolted us all momentarily out of our personal panic.

"What do we do?" I asked.

"We wait."

"But…," I started to say, but Teddy cut in again with "We wait. Listen. We can't move against Abbadon until we know more. We don't know if Niko is in trouble, yet."

"But…," I began again, but this time was cut off by Niko himself who whispered, "He's gone. He stopped the punishment from going too far and gave out orders for moving out.

"He didn't show a flicker of recognition. He looked just like his picture." As if talking to himself he added, "How can he look like a kind man and be such an evil monster?"

I thought back to the many times Sarah and Leif had talked to me about how the true monsters in the world hid behind the facade of goodness.

I missed Sarah and Leif and their wisdom. I knew they were back at the Castle making sure that whatever we did here didn't impact Zerenity negatively. So far we hadn't done much, but I knew that was coming to an end.

The next few hours were torture. My jaw ached from clenching my teeth together. I knew that Niko and Aki would not be happy with me if I didn't practice relaxing while we waited, so I would relax and then get tense all over again.

I wanted to be up and doing. I wanted to throw fire bolts, or fly through the trees striking down the raiders, or—well almost anything but lie there.

Aki, Niko, and Zeid would check in if something were wrong. Otherwise, they were to remain silent. Ruta hooted from the trees. Sometimes Teddy would say something silly, and we could hear Pita snort in response. But mostly we were quiet.

After what felt like five thousand years, but was just a bit shorter than that, Aki told us that she and her mother were on the way.

At the same time, Niko said the Raiders were within a hundred feet of the village. Too close. Much too close. If the Raiders saw Aki and her mother, they were lost.

Niko opened his channel for us to hear what was happening. I knew it was what we had agreed for him to do. But the screaming was terrible, and we were not able to do a thing to stop it.

The Raiders were yelling at the top of their voices, and the villagers were begging for mercy. Mercy that would never come. And we had agreed to let it happen. We could only guess what Niko was doing. We knew it would be the worst day of his life. He would be part of the Raiders that destroyed his village. He would be watching as the Raiders captured everyone including him and his sister.

What if this was a mistake? What if we should have stopped this before it started? I knew everyone was thinking the same thing, but it was too late. We had decided, and that decision meant we were all part of a tragedy that could never be undone. We would never forget it. It would haunt us for the rest of our lives. We all paid a price that day, but it was the people of Willowdale that paid the worst one.

Listening to the battle, praying that Aki and her mother were safe, knowing that we could have stopped the death and destruction going on, I promised myself, that we would end this or never go home again.

"Amen," Teddy whispered. Once again I had left my channel open to my private thoughts, but this time I was glad. I wanted to be held accountable. I was a Princess. I had power. I would use it.

"We're on our way," we heard Aki whisper, and the three of us breathed a sigh of relief as we stood, stretched our frozen muscles, and then moved silently in their direction.

The Raiders were busy with the village. Abbadon was heading back to his Keep where he would wait for his new prisoners.

We should be safe, but there was always the chance that he had spies in the woods that we didn't know about. After all, we were there, hopefully without his knowledge. So in a way, we were the spies in the woods.

Abbadon has his Raiders, but we had more help on our side then Abbadon could ever imagine. The trees, the rocks, the earth, all of nature was on our side.

The trees had spread the word that we were there to stop Abbadon's reign of destruction, and we could feel their support and encouragement.

As we started to move, I was so stiff I tripped over my feet. This time it was Garth who kept me from falling.

"Still clumsy, I see," I heard Ruta whisper, and the trees laughed.

Once again they had taken pleasure in raising a root for me to trip over. It worked. I stopped clenching my jaw and smiled instead. I had friends. Abbadon had hate.

From my time with the people in Doveland back in the Earth Realm I had learned that Love was the only power. We had that a hundred times over.

Thirty-Three

For the next few hours, there was no time to ask any more questions. Everything moved so fast it was a blur. After I tripped over the tree root, we ran towards Aki and her mother, Tarla.

Aki had told us that her mother had trouble walking and she could use some help. She assured us that no one had followed her from the village, but still, we were on the lookout for anyone that Abbadon might have sent into the woods as scouts.

That's what we would have done, but there was no one there. The fact that there wasn't, was almost more frightening. Why wasn't there anyone? Abbadon was smarter than that. It felt more like a tease. Perhaps he was making it easy for us so that he could be in control of us later. That's what it felt like to me, and I knew I wasn't alone in that feeling.

I had heard Ruta whisper, "This is too easy," and no one disagreed.

Still, we did our job. We found Aki stumbling towards the cave, holding a woman who, if she had been healthy, would have looked exactly like Aki.

Instead, she had scars running down the right side of her face, and her right leg dragged on the ground. I hissed at the sight. There was no question in my mind but that she had run across one of Abbadon's minions at some point. Garth hurried to Tarla's other side to support her weight, and Anne and I watched the woods for signs of trouble. There was nothing. Again, the lack of trouble worried me.

We made it back to the Cave without incident. Tarla was crying. "Are you in pain," I asked, as I helped her get comfortable. When I couldn't understand what she said I realized that Aki and Niko not only transformed themselves to look like us, but had also learned a new language. "She says she is happy to have escaped the Raiders. And she is worried. Her children are in danger," Aki translated.

"She doesn't know that you are her daughter? How did you get her to come with you?"

"I tried to explain, but it didn't make any sense to her," Aki said. "All she could see was Niko and Aki as tiny children getting carried away by the Raiders. She screamed. I screamed too. Both of me screamed. It was horrible." Aki stopped to catch her breath and look away from her mother for a moment.

Turning back to look at us she said, "How was I going to tell her that I was letting that happen? I couldn't.

"Instead, I ended up telling her that I was from another village, had escaped, and needed to rescue her to make myself feel better for what had happened with my village. It wasn't that far off from the truth.

"It took a long time. She was worried about her children and the rest of the village. She would only leave after she saw us getting carried away. I convinced her she couldn't do anything to help if she was captured too, and finally, she agreed to come with me."

Aki was holding her mother's hand and crying almost as hard as her mother. I had never seen Aki cry. The horror of what was happening was a hundred times harder for her than the rest of us. She was suffering in two timelines, and there was nothing I could do but listen and nod as if I understood. I understood, but I would never really know how that felt.

As Ruta worked on healing Tarla of her immediate pain, we asked Aki how they got away.

"It was Niko. He pretended to capture us and then he dragged us into the forest. At first, someone yelled at him that he was going the wrong way, but he told them he had plans for us."

Aki's breath caught in her throat. "They gave him the high sign. Good for him. He was taking what he wanted. We screamed to make it real. My mother's screams were real. Mine were almost as real. The whole thing was terrifying. Mom didn't know it was Niko. He was a Raider. He looked just like them."

"After a while, Niko whispered to us to start running, and he walked out of the woods to help capture more people. I heard people yelling at him to come help with the children. I know he did. It must have been terrible."

All of us hung our heads. What could we say? It was terrible.

So far we had not heard from Niko or Zeid. We didn't expect to until things had died down. The chance that someone might notice our open channel was too high. We would be switching every four hours to a new one from now on until we were done, but it was safer to leave theirs closed until they opened it again when they were safe.

We had laid Tarla in the back of the cave. Ruta's ministrations had calmed her down enough to sleep. We thought that probably she hadn't had a peaceful rest for many years. Seeing people she had never seen before, who spoke a strange language must have frightened her even more. Did she know she was safe?

"Will you be able to heal her leg, Ruta?" Aki asked.

"I made it stronger so she will be able to limp, but I am not sure I can take those scars away or completely heal the leg. Her mental trauma is so intense it is keeping me from doing a complete healing. Once this is all over, perhaps. But for now, that's the best that I can do."

Aki reached out and held Ruta's hand and then leaned over and kissed him. Ruta gasped and then smiled bigger than I had ever seen him smile. We all need praise. We all need to know that we are useful and needed. It's not that we aren't, it's that we yearn to be told.

The Priscillas still hadn't returned. And they had not checked in either. With no communication from them or Niko and Zeid, we were left to wait. Once Tarla woke, we would leave the cave and follow Pita and Teddy to the circles that would take us down to the tunnels where the next part of our plan would unfold.

That was assuming that the first part had gone well. We had Niko and Aki's mother. Now, we needed Niko and Zeid in place. And safe. Safe. We needed them to be safe.

I needed them to be safe.

Thirty-Four

Our plans changed after Tarla woke up. She was so terrified that we were afraid to move her. Besides we hadn't heard from Niko or Zeid. Scary enough in itself, so no one said anything. We didn't want to make it worse.

Aki spent most of the day sitting beside her mother holding her hand and sometimes speaking to her in their native language, which seemed to be helping. I wondered if Tarla would be able to accept that Aki was her grown-up daughter, or if Aki was going to leave it alone and not try to explain it again.

Anne and Garth sat together quietly. I thought they had plenty of practice observing where they were, instead of interacting. I needed to learn some of that skill. Instead of feeling like I wanted to punch a wall out, or at the very least complain about the waiting.

Teddy and Pita were monitoring our channel, and talking over something they were designing. They wouldn't share what it was because they said sharing ideas too soon was like pulling up flowers to see if the roots were growing.

The Priscillas still hadn't come back. Was I the only one worried about that? Aki looked at me and frowned. Okay, maybe not. Ruta had checked on Tarla one more time before heading outside, and then I imagined that he headed back up into a tree.

I seemed to be the only one who was having trouble waiting. I paced back and forth across the cave until Pita gave me a look and told me to stop it. By the look on everyone's face, they were all in agreement.

"Why can Ruta go outside and climb a tree and I have to stay in here," I whined. "What use am I in here?"

"Well, Impatient Girl," Teddy said, "You aren't. Why not go visit Ruta?"

Everyone in the cave tried to hide their pleasure at that idea, but I knew what they were thinking. Not only did they want me to leave them in peace, they thought it would be interesting to first, see me climb to the top of the tree, and second, bug Ruta with questions. Because they knew that was what I would do. I was, once again, filled up with questions. Could I do it? Could I climb the tree? Would I?

"I will then!" I said, trying to sound positive and ended up sounding childish. I turned on my heel and walked out of the cave hoping I looked dignified. But when I whacked my hand against the cave entrance and everyone laughed, I knew I had only succeeded in looking ridiculous. It was par for the course.

As soon as I stepped outside into the forest, I felt so much better. I could almost forget that we were in the middle of fighting a battle. A battle that the more I thought about it, the stupider it seemed to me, which is why I needed to get some questions answered.

Climbing the tree to get to Ruta would be easy once I got myself in tune with the trees because I knew they would help.

I stood waiting for a tree to call to me. Trees don't call out vocally, at least not to me. Instead, it's as if they send out a thought beam and it catches me and wraps around my heart and pulls me forward.

It didn't take long to feel that pull. I silently thanked the tree and mentally bowed before walking over to sit under the red maple that was only a few feet from the cave entrance.

Its leaves were beginning to turn. Soon the whole tree would be ablaze with bright red leaves. Every autumn I marveled at the ability of trees and plants to let go. They are not only letting go, but they are also giving. Every leaf provides as it transformed into soil, which in the cycle of life would support other life including other trees.

That thought helped ease my distress a little. I was holding on so tightly to our plan, I was blind to everything but that idea. Which then made me worried, or angry, and that just increased the cycle.

Thinking that a tree would never be angry because it was dropping leaves, I had to laugh, and the tree responded by dropping a shower of leaves onto my head.

At the same time, Ruta stepped out of the tree.

"I thought I would save you the climb," he said. "I understand the need to ask questions out loud to gain clarity. I often do that myself."

"I've never heard you do that."

"That's because you have never listened, or been available."

Seeing my downcast face, he added, "You're learning, Kara Beth. You are so much wiser than when you first returned. And it wasn't all that long ago. Besides, Beru has always been the one who listened and helped me figure things out."

"I'm sorry, Ruta. You must miss her as much as I do. I think that's what is making all of this waiting so much worse. Beru is always here for all of us. And Cahir. I miss Cahir.

"I worry that they won't be there when we get back. That we will do something that changes everything and then some. Or that all the people we love won't be there. It's actually more than worry. I'm afraid."

Ruta reached over and put one of his hands on mine. "We need that fear, Kara. But it can't let us become blind to what is going on, or be paralyzed by it. Which scares you more? That they won't be there or that you can't return?"

"That they won't be there. If I can't return, I could still hold out hope that they were still alive, or maybe see them in this timeline." I paused for a moment to hear what I had just said. "So, could we see Beru and Cahir in this timeline? Or any of the rest of our team?"

"We could if they are here. But that's the tricky part, isn't it? By seeing them here, we may end up being the cause of them not being in the future when we return to it."

"You're sharing with me aren't you, Ruta?" I asked smiling at him. "Thank you! Are you ready for all my questions now?"

Ruta nodded yes with the tiniest smile on his face, but before I could begin, the Priscillas came flying through the trees straight to my head. Both Ruta and I ducked. I tried to cover my hair, but Pris got a hold of it anyway.

"We have news! Meet us in the cave."

Ruta and I looked at each other and shrugged. I stood, offered a hand to Ruta, and the two of us walked into the cave together. I had a tiny bit of satisfaction at the amazed looks on everyone's face. Ruta holding hands?

But the Priscillas were ready to talk, so we made ourselves comfortable and prepared to hear their story.

Thirty-Five

They took their time. The Priscillas love a stage. They waited until everyone was ready, including a now awake Tarla who stared at the Priscillas with a smile on her face.

"She knows you?" I asked in bewilderment.

"She knows fairies," Pris replied and then flew over to Tarla and started talking to her in Tarla's native language. Soon the other two fairies joined them. All of them were babbling together waving their hands in the air. Aki talked excitedly to Pris while Tarla, La, and Cil smiled and nodded.

The rest of us looked on in amazement, waiting as patiently as possible for them to be done.

It was Aki who told us what they had been talking about after the conversation died down and Tarla looked more at ease than before. She was now leaning up against the cave wall, while Cil lounged on her shoulder. I smiled at Cil. I knew what she was doing. She had done it for me countless times. Calmed me down. Gave me courage.

"Mom didn't know the Priscillas, but she knows some of their relatives, and they were discussing the times they spent together. No, I had no idea that the Priscillas knew my native language or that they had known about my family. That, I know, is partially my fault. Niko and I never revealed our secret to any of you. Maybe we should have done it earlier."

Pris flew over to Aki's shoulder and kissed her on the cheek and whispered something.

"Oh, they knew all along, but chose to keep our secret," Aki said, crying again out of gratitude. First, she had her mother back, and now she knew how well she had always been watched over.

As Aki spoke with us, Tarla's face started to change, and when Cil said something to her, Tarla began crawling towards Aki. We didn't need to know her language to understand that she had finally recognized Aki. The crying and hugging lasted a long time. It raised all our spirits. We had accomplished one thing. We had reunited Aki with her mother. It was a win on our side.

There was much to do, and we had no idea what the outcome of what we had done would be. But at that moment there was pure joy in all our hearts.

****

"We still need to hear what the Priscillas have to say," Teddy finally said, breaking into the celebration that was going on. "And I know that Twinkle Eyes is still bursting with questions. Most likely ones that we better try to answer while we still can. So let's get on with it, people."

We all laughed. Pris retook center stage and began to tell us where they had been and what they had discovered. She had all of our attention, something I knew she loved. Cil remained on Tarla's shoulder to translate what Pris would say. It didn't take long for Pris to disrupt everything. In fact, it only took a few seconds and two sentences.

"As you have heard, some of our relatives also lived here during this timeline. So, we went to see them."

At first, we all gasped in horror wondering what that choice had done to the future. But then we looked over at Aki and her mother and realized that we were already messing with timelines by rescuing Tarla. And that wasn't even counting the fact that the adult Niko was now in the same place as his child-self. We were already playing with fire.

"I sure hope we know what we're doing," I mumbled to myself, and Ruta gave me a nod. I loved it, Mr. Grumpy agreed with me.

Pris continued, "I know. It might have been reckless, but we thought it was the right thing to do. Like the Ginete, we too don't have a problem viewing more than one timeline at a time."

Turning to Anne, Pris said, "How do you think we knew to come out of the forest at that time to save you from Abbadon?"

"Wait. Are you telling us that we are in some kind of time loop? You did this very thing before? Are you going to burst out of the forest again and punch Abbadon? What good will it do? Seriously, I don't get it."

Teddy shook his head and said, "I don't think any of us get it. But let's pretend that we do. Are you going to do the same thing again?"

Pris slapped her head and looked at all of us as if we were idiots. "Ziffer. No. We're here before we do it, or did it last time. That's why we chose this time. Or Suzanne did. If you think about it, when Anne tells Abbadon no, that would be the perfect time for us to capture him. He is out of control at that moment."

I was so upset that I stood up without thinking about it.

"Well, then why did we need to let Abbadon raid the village? Why did Niko and Zeid need to get to the Castle? Why did we do all that if we are going to capture Abbadon? And then, what the ziffer are we going to do with him? Assuming that your plan to capture Abbadon works.

"And wait, how will Zeid and Niko know what is happening. Didn't you change everything without telling us? Shouldn't we have known?"

The more questions I asked, the more upset I got. I was actually stamping my feet and trying to keep my hands from getting hot enough to release a fireball or two. I didn't think I was alone in feeling that way. Everyone else was looking at Pris as if she had lost her mind. Everything about the planning of the mission seemed entirely out of whack.

The Priscillas had made me frustrated before, but this time I felt like strangling them or at least pulling Pris' hair the way she pulled mine. Luckily for Pris, Niko came online just at that moment, and what he had to say was scarier than the Priscillas bogarting our mission and putting our future in danger.

Thirty-Six

Niko spoke quickly. "Zeid's here. The Raiders appear to have accepted us. Or at least they are giving us the impression that they have. It's hard to say if it's an act or not. There's not any camaraderie between them, so the fact they don't recognize us doesn't seem to matter.

"We think that there is something else going on here. We believe that after the men from the villages are captured, some of them, or maybe all of them, return as Raiders. We recognized at least one of them from the men captured at Willowdale. Maybe Abbadon does something to them to turn them into a Raider.

"The women, children, and older men are taken somewhere else. We haven't found that place yet. It's harder to sneak away then we thought it would be, so Zeid is going to have to do his vanish and reappear act more often than he wants to."

"Have you seen Abbadon?" Teddy asked

"The last time we saw Abbadon was at the Raiders camp. I know I keep saying this, but something seems very off about them. We have to act almost brain dead not to stand out. We wanted to let you know that we found out that we are to be going out on raids every day. And some of the places are located days away."

Before any of us could say anything, Niko added, "It's okay, we are not going. We'll figure out a way to remain here in Abbadon's Keep and explore the buildings. But you need to know that bands of Raiders are being sent out to search the local area, so it's time for you to get to the tunnels. Be careful. There are already Raiders near you. Abbadon must suspect something."

Zeid burst into the conversation, "Gotta go. Something is happening."

After that announcement, the channel went quiet.

We all stared at each other in horror. What was happening? Were they safe? Besides, we hadn't had time to tell them about what the Priscillas had done, and their hair-brained idea. But we couldn't worry about that. We had to get out of the cave and to the magic circles that would take us down into the land of Ginete and Whistle Pigs.

Aki said something to her mother, and she nodded and stood up. We grabbed our backpacks, put out the fire and did everything we could to make the cave look the same as when we entered it. The circles were about a mile away, and the Raiders could be anywhere.

"We'll go look," Pris said, as they flew away. Staying angry at them was hard. They were always looking out for all of us. Perhaps not in a way we would have anticipated, but maybe that was a good thing.

"We could travel through the overstory," Ruta said, "But I am not sure that Tarla could make it."

Ruta was referring to the time we were trying to avoid being seen by the people driven mad by the Deadsweep thought-worms and the trees had assisted us moving through the very top of their branches.

"No, we are going to have to walk it, and I am going to need help with my mother," Aki said. Although Tarla was looking better, she was still dragging her leg. She would need support on both sides.

Teddy took over the instructions. "Garth and Anne, could you please help Tarla? Aki, we are going to need your ability to come and go unseen to help the Priscillas in tracking the Raiders. Kara, are you ready with your bracelet? And of course your fireballs," he added with a chuckle.

Teddy loved it when I shot lightning out of my hands. True, it is a spectacular sight, but also dangerous for other things and I need to be careful not to catch a tree on fire or harm any innocent beings. The bracelet might be a better choice. I had been practicing with it, and Teddy knew that. He had seen Niko take me out time and time again to try to use it effectively.

The bracelet had been my mother's. She left it with Professor Link before going to Ruta's village and then dying there with the rest of the town when the Shrieks and Shatterskin attacked. She had told him to give it to me. I still didn't understand why she didn't take it with her in the first place. Perhaps she could have stopped the Shrieks and Shatterskin with it, or at least held them off while they escaped. I would never know the answer to that question, but I was grateful to have the bracelet

If I used it correctly, I could send a beam, or wall, of energy that stopped anything from moving. Although my intention was always to stun, if I didn't control the energy correctly I knew that it could kill. I didn't mind killing the machines or the mechanical thought-worms, but I didn't think that I could kill any living thing, even the Raiders.

Maybe especially the Raiders. If these were men taken from villages, how did they turn into heartless, vicious Raiders? Could we reverse the process?

Even before we had left the cave, Cil flew back in a frenzy and said, "They are all around you."

"Do they know we are here?" Teddy asked.

"We don't think so. They are walking through the woods just looking around. They don't appear to be looking for anything specific, like you …"

Cil's voice trailed off as her face grew pale. She cleared her throat, gathered herself, and added, "There is a tiny corridor between the teams of Raiders. If you are very quiet, we think we can lead you through it. Just follow me."

Cil glanced at me and pointed to her wrist and then her throat. I knew what she meant. I might need the bracelet, and I might also need to use the star to see 4D. I nodded in acknowledgment. I could sometimes see 4D without pressing the blue star necklace given to me by Liza, the young girl who lived in Kinver. But I couldn't control it. And when I felt stressed it was harder. I was definitely stressed.

We moved out behind Cil. Teddy led the way. Aki and I kept to the outside of the line, continually scanning, using 360 degree vision to see all around us. Ruta was behind Garth, Anne, and Tarla, and Pita was in front of them.

The Priscillas kept us up to date as to where we were going, and we were doing well moving quietly through the woods. Then Tarla coughed.

Thirty-Seven

The woods erupted with howls. It sounded as if hundreds of people were screaming at the top of their lungs. I had heard the phrase "screaming like bloody murder" but had never understood what that meant. Until that moment. The howls came from all directions, surrounding us completely. I had never heard anything like it before, and it sent cold chills up and down my spine and froze me in place.

I wasn't the only one frozen in place. Everyone looked as if a bucket of ice water had been thrown on them and the world had stopped. Even Teddy was frozen. What were we to do? The Priscillas flew back and jumped into the pocket of my tunic. So much for guidance from them.

I turned towards, Ruta. "Ruta, travel with the trees. Get to the circles. Aki, you go too since you can appear anywhere you need to. We'll try and also get there. But we can't all be trapped here."

"Wait," Pita said. "I have a better idea." He looked at Teddy who had snapped out of being frozen in fear and nodded at him. Teddy reached into his backpack and pulled out a package of netting.

I recognized it. It was the net they had used to throw over

the infected with the thought-worms to trap them.

"That's not going to work," I said. "There will be too many of them."

By then the howls were almost on top of us. We could hear the Raiders crashing through the brush, howling, grunting, screaming mindlessly.

"Everybody crouch down and be quiet," Pita said, as he and Teddy unfurled the net. We did what we were told even though I was sure we were soon to be trampled or captured or maybe killed by maniacs. But it was too late to do something else.

"Get out here and help," Teddy hissed at the Priscillas. Within seconds the Priscillas were holding the edges of the net and were dragging it over the top of us. As it passed over each person, they disappeared. Zut, it was making them invisible.

As the last of the net dropped over Ruta, we didn't need to be told to make sure that we were all covered. Not even the tiniest bit of our clothing could be sticking outside. We were invisible from the outside, but under the net, we could see each other. All our eyes were wide in terror. Would it work? I don't think any of us were breathing.

A horrible thought occurred to me. What if the Raiders stepped on us? Pita and Teddy shook their head at me, a tiny movement. I hoped that meant that the net also blocked anyone from coming into our space. When I thought that, Pita winked at me, his huge golden eyes half closed. Sometimes he reminded me of an owl. It was a random thought, but I needed something to keep from thinking about what was happening all around us.

The howls were right on top of us. They circled us and screamed louder and then I heard what sounded like a shout and they moved off towards the sound. We waited until everything was quiet, and then La crawled out from under the net and looked around. She crooked her finger at her sisters, and all three of them moved out, motioning for the rest of us to stay in place.

A few minutes later they were back, all smiles. How could they be smiling at a time like this? In fact, they were smiling at me. Why?

Pita and Teddy started pulling the net off of us and folding it into an impossibly small square. But my attention wasn't on them. It was on a movement near one of the trees. I grabbed Garth's arm and pointed to the tree, but Cil landed on my hand and shook her head.

"Not dangerous?" I asked.

I heard a low growl and looked again at the tree. Coming towards me was a wolf who looked exactly like Cahir. My mouth flew open, and I looked at the Priscillas who were dancing happily in the air. I looked back at the wolf and asked, "Cahir?"

"Yes," was the answer. I burst into tears and ran to embrace him. "You are Cahir from this timeline?"

He just shook his head. Did he not know what I meant, or he wasn't going to tell me? "You are the one who made that noise and pulled them away, weren't you?"

His answer was to nuzzle his head down into my lap. I hadn't realized how much I needed Cahir nearby. Until that moment I had told myself that it was okay, but it hadn't been. Now it was.

"Lovely to see you, Cahir, or not Cahir," Teddy said, "But we need to get a move on before the Raiders return."

Now that the raiders were gone we quickly moved to the circles. I knew Cahir wouldn't come with me into the tunnels. He didn't like being underground or in the air at all. I hugged him and said I would meet him later. He bowed and trotted off into the brush. Pita did something, and within seconds we were down into the familiar tunnels, in a transportation room that looked like all the other ones we had used in the future.

It wasn't surprising. The art of tunnel building had been passed down from these Whistle Pigs and Ginete.

That's the first thing we saw. A room filled with Whistle Pigs and Ginete we didn't know. But it didn't take long for us to feel comfortable.

The first thing they did was take us to their dining room where all the food we could eat was waiting for us. For the second time that day I burst into tears. I wished that I would grow out of that compulsion to cry at the drop of a hat because it was so embarrassing.

"It's not embarrassing, Princess," Aki said. "It shows us all how much you care."

I gave her a grateful look and then hugged Pita and Teddy who were standing beside us. "Once again, you two have saved us."

They both bowed and said with a laugh, "Our pleasure."

For a moment, all was right with the world. I would take that moment, because I knew what was coming next. Or at least I thought I did.

Thirty-Eight

I watched Tarla as she took in her surroundings. I could almost imagine how she felt. This morning she was in her village, among friends and family that she had known her whole life, and now she was surrounded by people and beings she had never seen before, and who spoke a different language.

Raiders had attacked her village, her children were kidnapped, and the daughter she knew as a little girl was now standing in front of her as a grown woman.

In spite of all that, I watched as she smiled and laughed at the people sitting near to her at the table. She kept one hand firmly on Aki's arm, perhaps trying to convince herself that all of this was real, and she wasn't dreaming. What would she remember when we were gone?

What would any of these people remember when we were gone? Would we be a story that they told, and did they expect to see us again and again? Did time loop around? Or would we finish what we came to do and never return?

"You'll make yourself crazy asking all those questions, Kara," Anne said, sliding into the seat beside me. "We've learned not to try and conjecture too much about the 'what if' of dimension travel. Time travel is different, I know, but the not questioning too much part is probably the best way to complete what needs to be done.

"Even in one dimension, and in a single time frame, choices change everything. Things we can't control. Every choice we make here is going to change something. But what if it is those choices that made the future that we all remember?"

"Okay, you know that you just made my point, don't you?" I smiled at her.

"Yes, and I also made mine. We were told to do what is the right thing to do. Do it the best that we can. The outcome is not up to us."

"Even though we are going to have to live with the consequences?"

"We always have to live with the consequences. Yes, once again, making my point and yours at the same time. As for right now, I say we enjoy this banquet of food supplied by people that knew we were coming, even though we hadn't been here before, but in this timeline we have."

Anne delivered that last line while smiling at me, knowing that she was driving me crazy. I started laughing and nodded. "You're right. Let's eat."

She was right. All we could do was our best, based on the knowledge that we had. I had to trust our intention to stop Abbadon from destroying the sentient beings that lived in the Erda dimension, and if we kept our focus on that, we would end up doing the right thing.

The future we left was already in disarray. Half the continent of what I knew as the United States in the Earth Realm had been uprooted and destroyed. If we pulled off our mission when we returned it wouldn't have happened. Whatever else we changed we would have to accept. Even the possibility that our friends and family wouldn't be there.

"Did you ever think that other people would be there?" Ruta asked me inside my head. "Like your mother and my family? If we stop Abbadon, he won't have destroyed my village. Perhaps that means we both find people in the future that we have already lost. It can work both ways. Maybe it will work in our favor."

Ruta was looking at me across the table, his face more serious than I had ever seen it. It's hard to tell what Ruta is thinking on the outside. I didn't call him Mr. Block Head for no reason. But inside that exterior was a huge heart, filled with love for his family and friends. I knew that. I wasn't sure everyone did.

Ruta and I talking alone like this was new. But I was grateful that we were helping each other as we missed our mutual friend, Beru.

I had been thinking of the answer to this question for a long time. "I hope that is what we find, Ruta. I want your village returned to you, and my mother returned to me. But I am afraid of who might not be there as much as I am hoping for those that might return."

Ruta wiggled his fingers at me, and I returned the sign. It was an abbreviated version of the handshake the three of us shared as our special handshake. I knew that both of us wanted more than anything that Beru would be waiting for us when we returned and we could do our full handshake together.

When everyone had eaten their fill—and in my case, more than my fill—Teddy cleared his throat and stood up. "We are grateful to our fellow Whistle Pigs and Ginete for this warm welcome. Thank you for preparing this space for us to stay as we prepare for the next part of the plan."

Garth raised his hand. Teddy acknowledged him. "As much as I am grateful for this lovely food, and a safe place to stay, don't we need to talk about the plan? Especially, the Priscillas' idea to capture Abbadon. And if we are going to do that, don't we have to get a move on if we are going to do it during his reaction to Anne's saying no to him?"

A general murmur of agreement went around the room.

"Yes. And yet, plans made without sleep, and without listening are not plans that tend to work well. So we are all going to take advantage of the rooms prepared for us and get some rest. We'll meet in the meeting room in six hours."

As much as I wanted to get moving, I had to agree with Teddy, and apparently so did everyone else because we all rose from our chairs and followed our hosts to our rooms without a hint of complaint.

Even the Priscillas were tired. By the time I made it to my room they were fast asleep inside the pockets of my tunic. Within minutes, I too was asleep.

It happened so quickly I wondered if there had been something in the tea that was helping us all sleep. I wouldn't put it past Teddy. If so, I forgave him. In fact, I was grateful. Without it, I would have spent the entire night tossing and turning worrying about Zeid and Niko. And the future. Whatever we did, it would change it.

But as Anne had said, that was true no matter what timeline or dimension we were in. It was always about saving the future.

Thirty-Nine

Six hours later our team met in the planning room. We all looked better. Once again clean clothes were waiting for me when I got up, and a shower had felt wonderful. I was sure everyone had the same experience because for people who were planning to take over a dictator, we looked surprisingly good.

Aki had left her mother in the capable hands of the Whistle Pigs. If all went well, Tarla would remain there until our mission was over. Once it was safe, she could return home to her village. Part of our plan had always been to rescue the people living in Abbadon's Castle, along with those imprisoned in his manufacturing plants or wherever else he had prisoners within his Keep, and return them to their homes. That would mean that Niko and Aki, as the small children of Tarla, would return to the village, too. What we didn't know was what that would mean to the adult Niko and Aki. Would they be the same ones we knew now?

But that future "what if" question was never going to be something we would know until it happened. We had to take a bigger view and stop the destruction of Erda.

Once again Teddy stood up at the front of the room to run the meeting. "I can tell you," Teddy said, "that I can't wait to turn this job back over to Niko. So the sooner we accomplish our mission, the sooner we can all go back to the lives we love."

"Here, here!" We all shouted as if we were English men in a bar. Then we laughed. We laughed for so many reasons. For what we said, for thinking our lives would be the same when we finished messing with the past, and because we were a long way from pulling anything off.

Teddy continued, "In the past, we had John with us questioning everything about our plans. It made us think them through carefully. Since he is not here, and Princess Pumpkin Seeds loves to ask questions, I think we should have her voice the questions in her head that are probably in ours too. Because in order to have good answers, we need good questions."

Everyone at the table nodded their heads in agreement. Even the Priscillas nodded. As I looked around the table, it struck me how small of a team we were. It was Teddy, Pita, Aki, Garth, Anne, and Ruta. Only seven of us. Of course, Niko and Zeid were somewhere within Abbadon's Keep. But back in our own timeline, we had left Professor Link, Beru, Sarah, Suzanne, Leif, Earl, and Ariel. Plus the four men from Kinver.

I sighed. "Yes, I have questions. I guess the first one is, can the seven of us pull this off? But since we are going to try anyway, I have other questions.

"First, I have more general questions that I think we should discuss, and then specific ones."

Aki broke in, "You're right Kara Beth. We are going to have to say yes to the first question. Can we pull this off? Yes, we can. And to the part of the question you didn't ask, 'Are Zeid and Niko going to be able to do their part?' Yes, they can, and will. Now that's settled, let's get on with the other questions."

We all looked at each other in agreement with what Aki had said. What else could we do? We needed to have no reservations about our abilities.

"Okay. So here are some general questions. What is Abbadon actually doing? I mean that in the big picture. We've asked that before. Why plan to kill off all life? What does it gain him?

"Then, what is he doing with all these people he captures? Is he really turning the men into the zombie Raiders? How? We know that in the future he is using beings of all kinds to fuel his machines with their essence. Is that what he is doing now or is he experimenting? Why? Yes, there are many why questions.

"And then what about these questions:

"What happened to make Abbadon decide to do this? We believe that he got progressively worse after Anne turned him down. Did he? Or was that just a temper tantrum that revealed what he already was, and had already been doing? If Anne would have said yes, would he have stopped his activities?

"Oh, and why does it seem that he is a regular man with kind eyes, and yet we see the damage he is doing, and will do, in Erda?

"And after all those questions, I have planning questions. Do we agree with the Priscillas that we should capture him? Why? How? As far as we know Abbadon has great magical abilities. How are we going to capture him, and keep him? And then what? What will we do with him? Kill him? Imprison him? Take him back to the future with us? If he is so brilliant, won't he escape?"

Taking a breath, I looked around the room and wondered if I had asked all the questions in my head. Seeing the look on everyone's faces, I decided that even if I didn't get them all asked that was enough for now.

"Well," Teddy said, "That was a great set of questions. Anyone want to try to answer some of them or at least one or two of them?"

It was Aki that spoke up. "I think most of these questions are going to be answered after we capture Abbadon. So I vote that we spend our time figuring out how to do that. I think that perhaps since the Priscillas brought it up, they might have an idea?"

Pris jumped off my shoulder and into the center of the table. "Indeed we do! Actually, we didn't come up with the plan, our relatives did. Or, maybe we did, and our relatives remembered what we did. Oh, phooey, we can't figure that part out now. What matters is, there is a way to get him. And then perhaps Teddy or Pita have invented some way to drag out of him all the answers to those questions you have."

Pris almost cackled as she said those last words. It made me almost afraid for Abbadon. Almost.

Forty

Throughout all our meetings, Anne and Garth had stayed quiet, just observing. So when Anne stood up, we were all surprised.

"Before you continue down this road, I have another idea. I've been thinking about it for a while. But when Kara Beth asked the question about Abbadon reacting after I turned him down, and I realized how much we don't know, then my plan seems like the better idea."

Garth looked up at his sister with a worried look on his face. He must have sensed what she was going to say because even before she said it, the word "no" was already forming on his lips.

"Instead of telling Abbadon no, what if I said, yes?"

As the room erupted, Anne held up her hand. "I know you don't like this, Garth, and the rest of you might think I'm crazy, but hear me out. If I said yes, and agreed to go to his Castle to live with him until the wedding, I can also say that I want my brother, and my best friend to come with me. That way, we have appeased his anger, and we have three more people in the Castle.

"If I can keep him in love with me, he is much more likely to tell me things that you are talking about instead of torturing it out of him. Why not let him tell me?

"I am not holding out hope that I can convert him. But what if I can divert him while you come up with a better plan than capturing a man who has magical powers that we can only guess at, and hope to turn him into someone that cooperates with us before our time runs out?

"And I guess, if my plan fails I suppose we could capture him, or if I have to, I could stop him myself."

Teddy was stroking his chin. Pita had closed his eyes. The Priscillas were standing in the center of the table staring at Anne. Garth had turned completely white, and his hands were shaking. Aki, Ruta, and I looked at each other, and Aki nodded.

"I like it. There are many issues to be worked out here, but the idea is good. As long as Anne is willing to put herself at risk, I think we have to be willing to support her," Aki said.

"Am I your best friend in this scenario, Anne?" I asked

"I thought that you would be. You could be, Hannah. That way there are five of us already in the Castle with Abbadon."

"It would be awesome to be your best friend, Anne. But now I have to ask all the questions this plan brings up, starting with, do you think Abbadon would know who I am? After all, my parents sent me away to be free of him, and now I would be going straight to the man they were trying to protect me from."

Ruta spoke up, "As far as we know, Abbadon in the past never saw you. Only his future self knows who you are. I, too, agree this plan might work. But there are obvious issues." Turning to Garth and Anne, he asked, "While you were here in the past, did you meet yourself? You two mentioned that you felt you had to leave. Why? Did someone tell you to?"

Garth and Anne looked at each other, puzzled by what Ruta had asked. Garth shook his head, but Anne kept thinking.

"I dreamed it. In my dream, I heard someone tell me it was time to go home. When I told Garth about the dream, he said he had felt the same way. We had to return.

"Maybe you dreamed it too?"

"Perhaps," Garth replied. "I certainly didn't need any convincing even though up until then we both loved it here. And I thought Anne loved Abbadon."

"I did," Anne whispered. "I saw his flaws, but thought they could be smoothed out with affection. I thought he had been isolated too long, and I would change that. But for some reason, the dream took precedence over what I was feeling."

Ruta nodded and looked at all of us. "Did someone come to Anne in a dream and tell her to go home and not marry Abbadon?"

"Are you suggesting that one of us told her to go home last time and she remembered it as a dream? Which implies that we were here before and it didn't work? And now we are back again to try something else." I asked.

Ruta didn't need to answer "yes" to that question. We all understood what he said.

"Putting aside that we don't remember doing this, even if the past Anne says "yes," we won't be the ones in the Castle. She will. The past Anne and Garth don't know what Abbadon is doing. We need to get the future Anne and future Garth into the Castle, meaning the ones sitting here at the table," I said.

"Exactly right, Hannah," Anne said. It was strange to hear Anne call me that, but she was right. I couldn't use my Erda name. "It will be me that tells Abbadon yes, not the past me. So we still need to send the past Garth and Anne home, but earlier than last time, and Garth and I need to take their place."

"But, what if what we are going to do makes it so that Anne and Garth don't exist in the future to come back here?" I asked, confusing myself with the question.

"That's the chance we have to take," Anne answered.

"So who told you to leave last time in your dream?" Aki asked.

Anne looked at all of us around the table as if trying to place our face. She returned to me and said, "I think it was you, Kara."

"Me? How could that be? I don't remember any of this? Could you be mistaken?"

"I could, but I don't think so. I remember thinking I had met you before the first time I saw you back in Kinver. But I couldn't place it."

"So that means we tried this once before and did the wrong thing. We sent you home, not knowing that it would inflame Abbadon. This time, we try something else?"

When Anne nodded I added, "Let's hope this is the last time."

Aki looked around the room and asked, "Does everyone agree?"

Everyone nodded including the Priscillas. They agreed so quickly I wondered if the idea to capture Abbadon had been a ruse all along. One that would push us in a different direction.

When Pris winked at me, I realized we'd been had. *Who is orchestrating this mission anyway?* I wondered. Maybe it's been them all along. I hoped they knew what they were doing, because I still felt as if we were stumbling around in the dark, and I had yet to see the light at the end of the tunnel.

Forty-One

An hour later, Anne, Garth, and I were ready to go to the village and into the home where the other Anne and Garth were staying. If someone saw us along the way, no one would know that it wasn't the Garth and Anne that they already knew. They would introduce me as a friend of theirs who had come to visit. How did I get there? Magical powers of transportation, I guess. In Erda, that ability might be accepted as normal. Besides, it was something I was hoping to learn how to do someday.

We were counting on the theory that Anne remembered the encounter as a dream because that is how I told her to remember it. Garth and Anne were coming along to get me into King's Watch and into the right house, and to be ready to take the place of the other Garth and Anne the moment they left, which, if all went well, would be immediate. The past Anne and Garth would leave through the portal that would bring them back to their own time. And hopefully, nothing would change once that happened.

Our Garth and Anne were not going to show themselves to their past selves unless it became absolutely necessary. Who knew what would happen if all four of them were in the same place at the same time?

Teddy reminded us that what we call time happens all at once, but seriously, does anyone understand that? And so what? It just seemed a bad idea to be in the same place at the same time. Even being in the same area at the same time seemed like a bad idea, but there was nothing we could do about that.

Before we left, I said that I hoped that just because the town was named King's Watch didn't mean Abbadon was always watching. Aki assured me that even if he was, I wasn't doing anything wrong. The only suspicious thing would be if someone saw Garth and Anne outside, but knew they were inside the house at the same time. Yes. I would call that suspicious.

"Or spies? What about spies?" I asked. "What if there are spies watching everything and they report to Abbadon what they see?"

Pris pulled my hair, and Cil pinched my leg since Beru wasn't there to do it.

"Stop the whining, Kara Beth. We'll be watching over all of you. If anyone should be afraid, it would be Anne and Garth."

Anne turned pale, and Garth glared at Pris.

"That's enough," Teddy said. "We have work to do. Tomorrow is the day that Anne tells Abbadon. After she says, "yes," she has to get herself, Garth, and her best friend, Hannah, who has arrived the night before, into the Castle.

"Can you do it, Anne?"

Anne nodded yes. After that, we spent time arranging what would happen next. Once we were in the Castle, we would find Niko and Zeid. We still hadn't heard from them, and all of us were trying to hide our fears that something had happened to them.

Teddy and Pita would remain in the tunnels waiting for directions. Tarla would be waiting for it all to be over so she could go home. Ruta would be moving with the trees. If we could get to a tree, we would find Ruta. The Priscillas said they would be watching and would get into the Castle on their own if they were needed there. To get Aki into the Castle, Anne said she would ask Abbadon if she could hire a seamstress to make her a dress for the wedding.

Anne told us not to worry, Abbadon would want to move quickly. Maybe so he could own her. Perhaps because he really loved her. Although it probably mattered to the part of Anne that had loved Abbadon, it didn't matter to the rest of us. We only needed every one in his Castle as soon as possible.

Our goal was to stop him from destroying the future. But first, we had to send a few people back to the future.

****

Cahir was waiting for us as we rose to the surface. Since the future Cahir had allowed me to see through his eyes, I asked this Cahir if I could do that with him. His answer was to look at me as if I had lost my mind and then said, "We are one." I didn't care if he meant that the past and future Cahir was the same one, or that he and I were one, or the whole of nature was one, I was just happy to hear his voice in my head.

"Questioning things again," Aki said, moving to my side. She was going to walk with us into town where she would set up a seamstress shop that would look as if it had always been there. Aki didn't look like herself. Again. If she hadn't spoken, I wouldn't have recognized her.

"Always," I answered. "And here's one for you. Were you born knowing how to do the magical things that seem to come so easily for you, or did you have to learn them?"

"We are all born with our gifts, Hannah. Our job is to

discover them and use them. But not everyone has all of them. All beings are unique, and yet we are all intertwined. As Cahir said, 'We are one.' Being a chameleon is a gift that belongs to my race of people. However, I still had to practice it, as you have to practice yours."

"I'm not so sure I know my gifts, Aki. They seem so unspectacular compared to the things that all of you do. Levitate, move within trees, shapeshift, disappear, and reappear at will. So far I can throw lightning bolts on my own. Everything else I have to use a tool, like my bracelet or star necklace.

"Teddy and Pita save us with their inventions, Earl and Ariel are the wind and the storm. Oh, and then there is Leif and Sarah, the wizard and the Oracle. Seriously, I am clumsy and not great at anything that you and Niko have taught me."

I turned to look at Aki and said, "I know I sound as if I am whining and I am a little. But mostly I am worried. What good am I here? What if I mess something up? I don't understand why I am of use here other than being the possible future Queen of Zerenity, which is not something I aspire to at all."

Anne and Garth had turned around to see where we were, and Aki held up her hand telling them to give us a moment.

"Sometimes it is hard to see our own value. But questioning it means you are challenging the infinite One who made us all. Not those two bored-brothers on a spaceship. They are not the creators. I am referring to whatever made us all to express Life. It is not yours, or mine, to figure out. It is yours to agree to participate and do everything you know how to do. No one thread in a tapestry is more important than another.

"When this is over, perhaps you will be able to look back and see how it only worked because you were there. Or that all of us were here together. Either way, this is no time to question your importance. As Cahir said, 'We are one.' What we can do is for the good of all, and that goes for all of us: even you, Hannah.

"Now let's get going. There is no more time for self-doubt. From this point on, you are Hannah, Anne's best friend. Be that, and all will be well."

Forty-Two

Thirty minutes later I was standing outside the door where Anne and Garth were staying. The past Anne and Garth. I was alone. The others were waiting for me behind a stand of evergreen trees. Aki was almost invisible, having made herself look like the tree. Well, almost like the tree. If I looked closely, I could see her outline. I fought off the urge to be jealous and ashamed of myself for not being able to do cool things like that.

What had Ruta said to me when I first met him? That I was too self-important. He was right, and I was still working on getting over it. I took one last big breath and knocked on the door.

Anne opened it without even asking who it was. Of course, in this timeline, no one knew of Abbadon the monster. Why be afraid of a knock on the door?

We had all planned out what I was going to say to get in the door, but it turned out that it wasn't needed. That was good because I was tongue-tied. It was hard to believe that it wasn't the same Anne who was now hiding in the trees. This Anne stared back at me and then gestured for me to come inside.

She closed the door and motioned for me to follow her. Wasn't I a stranger to her? Why was she letting me in without saying anything? Anne turned and put her finger to her lips. The universal sign to not say anything. I could do that. I was too afraid to speak anyway.

We walked down a long hallway to a room at the back of the house. Sitting at a small kitchen table was Garth. I sucked in my breath. Garth? I didn't know I was going to be talking to both of them. Anne shut the door, motioned for me to sit, and then asked if I would like some tea.

Still not speaking, I nodded, yes. No one spoke as Anne poured tea for the three of us and then sat down at the table with us. Taking a sip of tea, she carefully placed the teacup back on its saucer, and turned to look at me.

"Hi, Hannah," she said.

I had just taken a sip of tea, and it came right back out as I choked and held a napkin to my face trying to stop coughing.

"Sorry. I know I shouldn't have startled you that way. But, I figured you'd be along sooner or later. Does this mean it's time for us to go home?"

Still sputtering, I nodded. Garth took pity on me and started rubbing my back until I caught my breath.

"I don't understand. I thought I would have to explain myself, and then you would not remember what I said and think it was a dream. How do you know who I am and why I'm here?"

"Let's just say we've done this a few times."

"Done what? Been here? Done this? I don't remember it at all."

"You've met us in the future right?" Garth asked. "So you know we are dimension travelers. And of course, you know about the first time we came back here by mistake. But the future Anne and Garth don't have this memory because we have chosen to forget once we return home.

"Then if Abbadon hasn't been stopped, something brings us back to this timeline and all of you, and we do it again. We don't know why the rest of you don't remember. Maybe it's a time loop for you. All we ask, Hannah, is please, please, please make it work this time. We are tired of making this trip.

"We suppose people have told you over and over again that it is up to you to save the Kingdom. That's true. If we could tell you what you need to do, we would. But we don't know. We just know it's you who has to end up doing the right thing."

"You don't have any idea what that right thing is?" I asked. I wanted to burst into tears. This has all been because of something that I didn't choose? How could that be? Why couldn't I remember?

Anne must have read my thoughts because she answered, "Maybe you don't remember because you have to make the choice from a fresh point of view. Past experiences might get in the way. I promise you, that if we knew, we would tell you.

"I do think that what we have told you might be your burden to bear, for now, Hannah, or Princess Kara Beth. Yes, we know who you really are, we know you in the future too, remember? And something else that we have learned as we have watched you each time is that you have a pure heart. That might be all you need to hold on to."

Even though my voice was barely working, I forced out a question, "Is there anything you might tell me about Abbadon that could help?"

Anne and Garth looked at each other. "I know that there is something about him that I found I could love. Is it because all monsters have a piece of themselves that is lovable and it's gone wrong? Or is there something else going on? I wish I knew. We only get this far each time and then we are sent home. I think the answer is something you are supposed to find."

"Are we to leave now?" Garth asked.

When I nodded yes, they stood up, and each of them came over and hugged me. I wish I could say that I didn't cry, but I did. These were two people I had come to love, and now I knew why. I had known them for a long, long, time.

"I'll see you two soon," I whispered.

"To the future," they both answered and slipped out the back door to return to their future. I prayed it was still there.

Forty-Three

We spent the night in our new home in King's Watch. I chose not to tell Anne and Garth what I had learned from their past selves. It seemed as if it was my burden for now, and it only would confuse the issue. All that we needed to think about was convincing Abbadon to bring us all into the Castle. Today, if possible.

Anne was sure she could do it. All she had to do was say "yes." All I had to do was recognize my choice and make the right one.

While we waited, Anne kept fiddling with her hair. Somehow Aki had managed to give her long hair again. I suppose it felt weird to have all her hair back after wearing it short for so long. I hoped the magic spell didn't wear off in the middle of the mission. Just one more tiny thing for us to put into the "let's hope it doesn't happen" pile.

That afternoon Anne went for her walk with Abbadon. Pita's relatives followed her just as they had in the past. The Priscillas were watching from the trees, along with a few of their relatives. All of that in case something went wrong.

Garth and I waited in the house practically biting our nails in anticipation. Cahir was in the woods, unseen by Abbadon, and was allowing me to watch what was happening. Sometimes he wasn't watching the road where they were walking though, and I had to ask him to turn back and watch Anne and Abbadon.

At first, I tried giving Garth a play by play description but that started driving both of us crazy, so I stayed quiet. Really, all we wanted to know is what happened when she said "yes."

As I watched, I was amazed by how happy Anne looked. Was she that good of an actor? She looked as if she was in love, and the Abbadon I saw walking with her seemed as happy as she. How could that be? I knew that if she said "no" he would turn into an abuser to her, and even more of a monster to the rest of the world.

I watched Abbadon turn to Anne, take both of her hands in his and then kneel holding up a ring. The perfect romantic picture of a proposal. I was astonished to discover that tears were running down my face. If I forgot who he was, I was so happy for them. I saw Anne nod, yes, and the two of them embraced, and Abbadon held Anne's face in his hands and kissed her gently on the lips.

What? Abbadon? What was going on?

My tears gave it away to Garth, and he fell silent. It was his sister who had put herself into the hands of the man we had come to destroy. I wasn't sure if we were more worried that she would be happy, or that she wouldn't be. But there was nothing for us to do except wait for the invitation to join Anne in Abbadon's Castle, or was it his lair? At this point, the only one who knew for sure was Abbadon.

Later I would think back to that moment and realize that it wasn't only Abbadon who knew. And the fact that we didn't have all the information is what made everything else that happened after that even more dangerous.

Instead, we sat there drinking cold tea and hoping for the best. Instead, it was the worst that was coming.

****

We didn't have to wait too long, although it felt like an eternity to the two of us. An hour later there was a knock on the door. I opened it as if I didn't have a care in the world, but I was as tense as a tightly wound guitar string. I thought if someone touched me, I might vibrate and play a note that sounded like panic.

Instead of Raiders, or Abbadon himself, a fresh-faced messenger from the Castle stood there. He handed me a note embossed in what looked like gold leaf. Abbadon and Anne were inviting us to come and stay at the Castle while they planned their wedding. Seeing both their signatures on the invitation made my head hurt. I felt pulled between terror and happiness for Anne.

A few young boys were standing behind the messenger carrying what I might have called duffel bags if I was in the Earth Realm. These were much more elaborate, but it was the same idea.

The messenger said that Anne asked me to pack what she would need at the Castle, along with what Garth and I wanted and the boys would bring it with them. We wouldn't be returning to the house.

I invited the messenger and the boys in and while they waited in the living room, Garth and I packed. "They look so normal?" I whispered to him.

"What were you expecting, gargoyles?" Garth whispered back.

"Well, maybe."

What was I expecting? So far none of what had happened was something I expected. Perhaps that was the way it worked. Abbadon sucked us in with normalcy. If marrying a King and living in a castle was normal. Still, it kept throwing me off balance. I expected to be wary and angry, and that was not what I was feeling. Except for it all felt wrong somehow. Too accommodating. Who was fooling who? Were we deceiving Abbadon or was he fooling us? Did he know what we were doing? Maybe this had all been a trap from the beginning.

Perhaps the spider had woven his web, and his prey was walking right into it.

Forty-Four

Along the way, we met Aki, who had also received an invitation. We greeted each other as if we had just met, and Garth nodded to her and thanked her for making his sister's wedding dress.

The messenger told us that Castle was a few miles out of town, and since the young boys were carrying our bags, there was nothing to keep us from enjoying ourselves, other than useless worrying. The road wound gently up and down hills, and alternated between being lined with trees and then opening to a view of the meadows. It was hard for me to imagine that anyone would want to destroy this beauty in exchange for a barren landscape with only himself left in it. But if what we had seen in the future was true, that was precisely what Abbadon intended to do.

I decided that during the walk to the Castle, I would not try to project what was going to happen, even a few hours into the future. I would simply enjoy the beauty. As I relaxed, I could feel Garth let go of some of his tension, and Aki turned and smiled at me. The woman she had chosen to look like had long dark hair that swung straight and shiny to her waist. As this woman, Aki was very substantial, not at all like her true transparent self or even the way she looked to us back in the Kingdom of Zerenity. Her smile remained the same, and her eyes were still pale blue. I wondered if it wasn't possible for her to change her eye color.

"It's not," I heard her say. "But I can change it temporarily which I will do once we get to the Castle."

"What about the boys and the messenger?"

"I already showed them brown eyes, although I doubt if they will remember me. It's you that they are looking at."

I glanced over at Aki in shock. "What are you talking about?"

"You haven't seen yourself in a mirror for a long time have you, Hannah?"

I shook my head and looked down, denying what she was telling me. And then it occurred to me that perhaps I could use it to my advantage. I wasn't going to rule it out. I didn't have enough magical powers to give up any advantage.

Even though I had determined not to worry while we walked, it was hard not to. We hadn't heard from Zeid or Niko. Assuming, hoping, that they were still in the Castle, what would they say when they saw us walk in?

Would they understand what was happening? Could we see them without giving anything away? I wanted to see Zeid so much I was afraid it would show. As for Niko, I had no idea what he looked like at the moment. He said he looked like a Raider. That in itself was terrifying.

Cahir kept showing me that he was following us. Since trees surrounded us, I knew that Ruta would be nearby, and of course, the Priscillas would be flitting in and out watching over us as we traveled. Below us were the Ginete and Whistle pigs. If we needed the circles, we would be able to see them. Until then they would be invisible. We were safe, and we weren't alone. It just felt that way.

As we reached the top of one of the hills I could see the Castle in the distance. I involuntarily drew in a breath. It was beautiful. Sitting gracefully on the rise in the middle of a meadow it gleamed in the sunlight. Flowers of all kinds greeted us as we walked the road that led to it. To our right was a massive expanse of tall sunflowers waving in the wind. I could see, and hear, birds enjoying the seeds. The whole meadow was pulsing with life.

As we drew closer to the Castle, I could see some of the buildings that we had determined must be where Abbadon took his prisoners and did whatever he did with them. We saw no sign of the Raiders. Abbadon's Keep looked like a small village filled with little gardens and beautiful trees.

There was no way I could reconcile what I thought of Abbadon, and knew of what he had done in the future, with what I was seeing. I knew that Aki and Garth were having the same problem. If the intent was to disorient us, it was working.

As we moved closer, enormous front doors swung open, and Anne stepped out into the sunshine, dressed in a beautiful green gown, and looking radiant. How could she? Wasn't she a little afraid? I had no time to think further because Anne ran towards us and soon we were all hugging her and congratulating her on her engagement and upcoming wedding.

I wanted to ask her so many questions I thought I would burst, but her whisper in my ear, "not now" stopped me from showing the slightest emotion other than joy for my friend.

As we stood there, a band of men came around the corner. In the middle of them was Zeid. I would have recognized him anywhere even though he wore the clothing of a Raider, and was walking in the same aggressive and slurred way of the raiders. These two attributes may seem to be opposite, but they aren't.

Instead, they create a picture of uncontrollable danger. Someone had designed that walk for them—someone who understood the power of movement.

These men were the first sign that things were not as Abbadon had wanted us to believe. Were they there by mistake or were they there as a warning? Zeid stumbled when he saw us, and I had a coughing fit to hide my distress.

The only thing I could think of was that at least he was still alive. Aki patted my back to help me with my coughing and managed to whisper that she had also seen Niko.

I caught her eye. She too was wondering if our seeing them was planned or an unfortunate incident on Abbadon's part. It could have been a coincidence, but none of us believed in those. It was a warning and confirmation.

But who was sending it to us? Were they on our side, or against us.

Forty-Five

Anne led us through the halls of the Castle, giggling like a school girl showing off her favorite new toy. Inside it was surprisingly like the Castle in Zerenity, and I wondered if the same architect had designed and built them both. If that was true, then at one point Abbadon and my father Darius must have known each other better or at least were willing to share information.

Although it looked similar, it had to be different. But the more I tried to find differences, the more it looked the same. What was different was how it felt. In the Castle at home, I felt warm and safe. This one was unsettling, definitely not warm and safe.

Anne led us to our rooms which were right beside each other. When the messenger who had stayed with us during the tour wasn't looking, Anne showed us connecting doors between our rooms, hidden behind bookcases. Who put them there? How did she know they were there? Why were they there? Were there doors in our rooms back in Zerenity and I hadn't known they were there?

I had enough questions to fill up the next few hours if there was only someone to answer them. How could this Anne know the Castle so well? Had she been there before, and if so, why hadn't she ever told us? Did this mean we had gotten this far before and failed? All signs pointed to that being true.

"Dinner will be in an hour," Anne said to the three of us. "You'll find clothes and everything you need in your rooms. Someone will come to escort you to dinner. I'll see you there!"

With one last hug for all of us, and a sweep of her dress, she was gone, but the messenger stayed behind, and then was joined by two more. Each one stationed outside our doors. Now that was different. And much more of what I expected. Now it made sense why Anne had shown us the connecting doors.

As soon as I closed my door, I heard it lock from the outside. I remembered Beru locking me in my room when I first came to Erda. I had long ago learned how to unlock a door, but there was no reason to give that secret away. Perhaps it meant they had no idea who we were, or maybe they did and that was why the door was locked.

Everything we knew had two sides to it. Which side was real? We were in the middle of a puzzle. One that had to be solved as quickly as possible. The longer we stayed in the past, the more danger we were putting ourselves and the future in. After the doors closed, Aki, Garth, and I met briefly in my room since it was in the middle of the other two. We agreed to use the dinner to observe, and not do anything that would draw attention to ourselves, or put Anne in danger.

An hour later, freshly showered, and dressed in the clothes left for me on the bed, I was ready when someone knocked on my door. Aki and Garth were already in the hall. We were all dressed as if we were going to a ball. Although it might have been innocent that Aki and I wore dresses instead of our regular tights and tunics, it didn't feel that way.

"How do people breathe and move in these things anyway?"

I whispered to Aki.

"They don't. I think that's the point," she answered.

The young man sent to get us led us to an atrium that looked very much like the one in our Castle in Zerenity. However, instead of metal toadstools delivering the food, it was men dressed like the one who came to get us. I tried to start up a conversation with one of them, but I got no response. During the dinner, I tried again, but the same thing happened.

The metal toadstools were more responsive than they were. The thought that they too might be machines made to look human flashed through my mind. My whole body must have reacted because Anne asked what was wrong.

There was no one else at the table. Just the four of us. A huge production. No other people. But every moment that we sat there I felt as if a thousand eyes were trained on us. Anne smiled, and laughed, and made light conversation, but we said nothing of importance.

I answered Anne with a laugh. "Oh, nothing. This is lovely Anne. I know I was hoping to meet your future husband and congratulate him. Will he be joining us for dinner?"

I gestured at the empty chair next to her. As soon as I asked the question, there was a disturbance on the other side of the atrium, and I could see the man we knew as Abbadon making his way towards us.

Once again, I was struck with how ordinary he appeared. Did he look like my father? Not really. Darius held himself like he was a King. He was sturdily built. Tall, with steel gray hair he kept short. He was always running his hands over his head. He rarely wore a crown because he would continually knock it off. But he didn't need it. In his prime, my father radiated power. Not the kind that scared, the kind that made his people feel secure. His dark eyes spoke of wisdom lived and practiced.

Not Abbadon. He looked more like the tradesman he had portrayed when he infiltrated our Castle. It was as if he wanted to look average. He too had steel gray hair, but he wore it longer, so a lock fell onto his forehead. He also had dark eyes. Eyes which others had said were kind. However, the closer he got to me, the more I thought differently. I thought his eyes were blank as if a screen had been drawn over them.

I had never heard Abbadon speak. I suppose I thought it would be a booming voice like Earl's, full of unmistakable power. So when he spoke for the first time, I was surprised again. My expectations were completely thrown off. It was soft, and to me, sounded ingratiating.

"I am so glad you could make it. My Anne has spoken of the three of you so much. Of course, I know you, Garth," Abbadon said, grasping Garth's hand in both of his. Inside myself I hissed. The first hint of the need to control had shown itself.

Abbadon bowed to Aki and kissed her hand, and then turned to me. It took every ounce of self-control to tilt my head to him and say, "I am so happy to meet you."

Abbadon lifted my hand to his lips, and said, "Not as happy as I am to meet you."

It wasn't the words that froze me to the core. It was the pulse that passed through my body like a warning signal, and the brief flash of his eyes as they came alive. I was the mouse being hunted by a hawk.

He knew who we were.

Forty-Six

We met late that night in my room. Although we knew it was possible we were being watched, we had no choice. We had to see each other and decide what to do next. We had all made it look like we were asleep in our beds just in case someone was watching, and Aki placed an invisibility shield around us as we talked. Another one of her hidden skills. Envy of Aki tried, once again, to take over my feelings, but it paled in contrast to my growing terror that we were now all prisoners of Abbadon.

He had us exactly where he wanted us. It was as if it had been his master plan all along. Do all those horrible things and then the only choice we would have would be to come back in time and stop him.

"It's an interesting theory, Hannah," Aki said.

It was strange to hear people call me Hannah again, and I realized that I didn't like it anymore. I was no longer the girl who had been sent to the Earth dimension. That girl had faded in my memory. I was Kara Beth of Erda. I couldn't wait to return to being called that. Even Princess Kara Beth felt better to me than Hannah.

For a moment the longing for all of this to be over and to return to our own time overwhelmed me and tears rose to my eyes. "Will we be able to get out of here, Aki, or are we trapped?"

Aki grabbed me by the arms and stared into my eyes. She might not have looked like the Aki I knew, but she felt like her. "Stop it. This is not how it ends, with us trapped in here. Remember he is alone, and we are a team with many skills. And we have strength of character. We have no choice. We have to stop Abbadon and return home. Do you understand?"

I nodded mutely. Aki was right. I had to pull myself together. If not for myself, for everyone that was counting on us to succeed.

I knew that if Beru were with me, she would have pinched me by now, or given me a look that told me she was disappointed in me. I thought back to the first few days of my training and remembered something that didn't make sense.

"When Beru first told me about Abbadon, she called him the Evil One. She also told me that he looks different than he used to. And that seeing him is a death sentence. Her exact words were, "Only a few have managed to escape. Even then, they rarely live for long after that.""

The three of us paused, and it was Garth who said what we were all thinking, "Then we haven't seen Abbadon yet."

A knock on the door froze us all into silence. The knock came again and a whisper, "I'm coming in. It's me, Niko."

I wanted to fling the door open, but Aki and Garth shook their heads, no. It could be anyone imitating his voice. Only Aki would know if it was really him. For a moment, Aki disappeared and then reappeared, smiling this time. Niko came in a second later.

After hugs all around we asked why he didn't do what Aki just did. Appear inside.

"Didn't want to scare the ziffer out of you," he answered

with a smile in his voice.

It was true. If he had come in the door either by opening it or appearing inside without opening it, we might have tried to hurt him. He had transformed himself to look like one of the young men guarding our doors.

"You figured it out. You're right. You haven't met Abbadon. That man calling himself Abbadon is one of Abbadon's creations."

"You mean he is like a robot? A machine?"

"Some of the people and beings you have met are that. Like the men serving you food. Others are real men, and some women, who have been modified to do his bidding. The man you see as Abbadon is one of those men. He has a few Abbadon duplicates. Some of them are better than others. The one you met at dinner seems to be his favorite. Maybe because he appears the most like him?"

All three of us stared at Niko in terror. "He can modify people to do his bidding? How do we recognize who is a machine and who is a modified person? And will they ever be changed back?" Garth asked.

As Garth finished asking that question, we heard a rustling in the corner of my room, and three of us turned prepared to fight. I was preparing to flash lightning bolts, and Niko and Aki were ready to pounce. Niko had pushed Garth behind him, to keep him safe.

To our amazement, Pita appeared in the corner of the room, the blue ring around the circle that brought him up disappearing within seconds.

"What the zonk!" Aki whisper yelled. "We were ready to blast you to kingdom come!"

"But you didn't," Pita said solemnly.

"How long has that circle been there?" I asked.

"Not long. We built it after we figured out which room you were in. We could take you all out of here now if you wish."

"It's tempting, but we can't go. We got in here, and we can't waste it. Now we have to find the real Abbadon and shut him down," Aki answered

We filled Pita in with what we had learned so far, and what we needed. He listened with his whole being. His lighthouse eyes fully open as if he heard with his eyes too.

Addressing Niko, he asked, "So, you think that some of the people you see here are machines, and some are people that are being controlled by Abbadon. But you can't always tell the difference, and you don't know how he is controlling them."

"That's about it. We also don't know where the real Abbadon is, or what he looks like. He may be disguising himself as one of his captives, or he could look like the monster that he is. We don't know."

"Can you capture one of them that you think is a machine and one you believe to be a manipulated person and get them to us?"

Niko nodded, "No one pays much attention to the Raiders, which I believe are men he has captured from villages. And perhaps I can get one of the table robots. Where do I bring them?"

Niko and Pita made arrangements based on a place in the Keep that Niko said was well hidden. As he turned to go, I asked, "Why aren't we using the channels anymore? We could have told you we were coming, and I need to know that Zeid is safe."

"I don't think our channels are safe, Kara. I shut them all down. I can hear your thoughts when we are close, but other than that we have to do this without our channels being open. And I forgot to give this to you, Kara." Niko handed me a piece of paper folded up so small I could barely see it in his hand. I grabbed it and retreated to a corner of the room to read what it said.

Turning to Pita, Niko said, "I'll be there within the hour."

To the rest of us, he added. "Don't go anywhere. Stay here. At the moment it's the safest place for you."

Forty-Seven

I never noticed Pita or Niko leaving. All I could look at was the note in my hand. It was a tiny scrap of paper folded over and over again. I knew Zeid had folded it that way to keep it hidden from the ever-present eyes. I opened it slowly, treasuring every moment of the unfolding process, careful not to rip it. Finally, it lay open in my hands, with the most beautiful words I had ever read written on it. It said, "I love you, Kara Beth."

Of course, I knew that. Zeid had shown me in countless ways how precious I was to him, but seeing the words, and knowing how careful he had to be to write them, overwhelmed me with gratitude and love for Zeid. I carefully folded the paper again and tucked it into the pocket of my leggings. We had all traded our fancy ballroom clothes for our own clothes as soon as we had returned to our rooms, grateful that Anne had told us to bring our things to the Castle.

This note was the exact opposite of the one I had found on my bed after we discovered the man we thought to be Abbadon had left the Castle. His note had said: "See you soon, Princess Kara Beth. To our future together, Abbadon."

"Sorry, Abbadon, we don't have a future together," I said under my breath. I was looking forward to saying it to his face.

Garth and Aki were sitting on the floor, waiting patiently for me. I wiped away my tears and joined them.

"I have a question, Aki."

Aki tilted her head to the side and waited.

"It's about the story you told me a few days after I returned to Erda. The one about the two bored brothers traveling in a serpent-shaped space ship through the galaxies. You said they had been traveling for eons and were looking for adventure. Although the rules of their civilization were that they could only be observers of other planets, and never instigators, these two brothers decided to risk the punishment. I guess they were so bored they didn't care what happened to them.

"They decided to run an experiment, like a bet between them. At first they were going to pick two planets and mess with them, but in the end, decided it would be easier if they picked one planet and used two dimensions instead.

"Am I on track so far?"

Aki nodded, and Garth had closed his eyes to listen. I wasn't sure if it was because he knew the story, or had never heard it before, but I continued.

"The planet they picked was this one. Gaia. The two dimensions they picked are the ones we call Earth and Erda. Although I know there are more, as Garth and Anne can tell us, these are the only two these brothers picked to do their experiment with on this planet."

"Lucky us," Garth mumbled.

"I remember you telling me, Aki, that the brothers seeded each dimension with people and beings that they had captured from other planets or universes. I suppose it was the ones that could live on Gaia. Then they started setting up the parameters of their 'game.'

"Have I got it right so far?" When Aki nodded yes, I

continued.

"Because they were not staying on Gaia, the brothers set up two other men, who were also brothers, to take their place in Earth and Erda. They made them different. How they made this happen is something I want to know, but I'll continue with the story first. They made one brother kind and generous and the other brother greedy and jealous.

"In the Earth Realm they were Cain and Abel, and Cain almost immediately killed his brother. This resulted in greed and envy being part of the fabric of life, which the kind and generous people in the Earth dimension try to overcome. In the Erda Realm, the brothers are Abbadon and Darius.

"There were some major differences in how they set up Erda. First, the people were allowed to remember their gifts, which on Earth would look like magic. In Erda, other beings are acknowledged rather than relegated to myths, or even worse killed. In Erda, the brothers were placed far apart. In Erda people don't consider age a "thing" because they view time differently, so the original brothers are still alive. Unlike in the Earth dimension where the people alive today are descendants of the original Cain and Abel."

Garth and Aki were listening to me carefully, and I caught a glimmer of pride on Aki's face. Her student just might be becoming awake.

"Now, here are my questions and I think, Aki, that the answers may be in the part of the story I don't know, and I think that you do because you hinted that you did when you first told me the story. If not, I hope that the three of us can figure it out."

Aki nodded, and Garth looked at her with hope in his eyes.

"I can see how keeping the brothers far apart held the peace for a long time. In the Kingdom of Zerenity, peace has reigned all these years. But, then one day, for some reason, Abbadon decides that his part of Erda is not enough for him. However, he doesn't just want to kill his brother. After all, what fun would that be?

"So he plots and plans and decides to kill everything. He makes machines, captures people and turns them into his slaves, and as we know eventually intends to destroy all sentient life. Why? What changed? And why would he want to be the only life left? In the end, he wouldn't survive either.

"So, there must have been something else that was different between Earth and Erda that has caused this. And although I have a feeling there is no logical answer or any way to find out, what were the bored-brothers betting? What would constitute winning?"

I looked over at Aki. "Did I get the basics right?"

She nodded and looked away. Sighing as if she had made up her mind, she turned back and looked at the two of us.

"You forgot one question, Hannah." Seeing me flinch, she said, "Okay, Kara Beth. Might as well say your real name now because obviously, he knows who we are."

Although I realized that was true, my whole body froze in terror. Then hearing what Aki said next, that terror sparked into abject fear and a wave of anger so big I barely heard what she said.

Forty-Eight

"The story I told you was told to me by Abbadon. That's how I knew it," Aki whispered, looking us both straight in our eyes and at the same time pinning us both to the floor with one of her magical tricks.

I knew why she did that, because otherwise I would have reacted and probably have done something stupid.

Garth looked as if she had slapped him. That's what it felt like. The person we had trusted the most had betrayed us. Could things be worse than that?

Aki waited for a beat and then said, "I have you pinned down because I was afraid you wouldn't let me finish. Are you ready to listen?"

I nodded, but I knew my face was broadcasting a combination of despair, betrayal, and anger. Aki released the hold on us, and now I had to contain myself. It wasn't easy.

"Ask your questions," Aki said.

"Really? Do I have to ask? You knew Abbadon. Correction, know Abbadon? When did you meet him? Do you know the real Abbadon or one of his minions?"

As I asked that last question, Aki raised her hand to stop me.

"See, I knew you would get to the heart of it. Was it the real

Abbadon? But let me start by answering your first questions. The man I thought was Abbadon told me the story when Niko and I were children and captives in this Castle. For all I know, an Abbadon is telling my child-self that story right now.

"I thought he was telling me a fairy tale. Especially since he started it the same way I had started it with you. Once Upon A Time. I was crying, missing my mother, and he found me huddled in a corner trying to become invisible. He gathered me up, gave me some water and a bit of food, and then asked me if I wanted to hear a story.

"Of course I did. I didn't know that was Abbadon then. I just thought it was a kind man who took pity on me. I tucked the story inside myself, and told it to myself over and over again, often wondering who that man was who had told it to me—wondering if it were true.

"It wasn't until the picture of the man we were calling Abbadon was shown to me after we defeated Deadsweep that I remembered the man. But it was almost impossible for me to reconcile that monster we were chasing with the man who told me the story.

"Then Anne and Garth came along, and Anne said she had felt love for the man she knew as Abbadon, and I began to accept that it must have been the same person."

Garth and I looked at each other, our anger gone. Instead, a glimmer of hope began to stir within me. Maybe the man that Aki had met told her something we could use now.

"Or maybe it was someone who looked like the man who told you the story," I said.

Aki nodded. "Yes, now that we know that Abbadon creates many replicas of himself, or what he wants to look like, I don't know if it was the same person. But that man came back a few times, always bringing water and food for me and then for

Niko, so he saved our lives.

"And now that we are here, I realize he must have known what was going to happen. Somehow he knew that we would return as adults, and attempt to stop the real Abbadon, and if I knew the story, I would know what to do."

"And now we are back to these questions," I said. "What changed? Or did nothing change? Perhaps the real Abbadon has always been plotting against life. So who is he? What was the difference that changed everything?"

Before Aki could answer my question, the door blew open, and a band of Raiders burst into our room. Abbadon, or an Abbadon, was with them. He didn't say anything. He leered at us as the Raiders grabbed us, pinning our arms behind us, and dragged us from the room.

None of us resisted the Raiders. Without speaking, we knew that we would be safer with the Raiders than with the man we knew as Abbadon. Besides, we had to find Anne before we began to fight. As they dragged us down the hall, we could hear laughter. It was coming from the walls.

I thought back to how the roots of trees lit walls and provided energy in Zerenity. Perhaps Abbadon used the tree roots to spy on everyone all the time. Aki turned her head and winked at me, a small smile on her face, which she quickly turned into a mask of fear and terror.

We knew something that Abbadon didn't know. At least we hoped he didn't know. Ruta was with the trees. If Abbadon was using the roots to spy on us, Ruta was doing the same thing. Besides, Pita and Teddy would be working with the Circles, and the Priscillas were out there somewhere. I knew them. They were always coming up with something unusual that would be just what we needed.

All those thoughts sustained me as we were dragged out into

the gardens of the Keep and into one of the buildings. In spite of my hope that we were not alone, the screams coming from behind the closed doors as the Raiders pulled us through the hallways of the building ate into my brain.

What was he doing to them? Where were we going? Did Zeid and Niko know where they were taking us and would they get us out? All my hopes were pinned on them until the Raiders opened a door and threw us into a room. After my eyes adjusted to the dark, I saw them. Zeid and Niko huddled in the corner looking terrified.

And lying in Niko's lap were three fairies. Not moving. I screamed and ran towards them, tripping over legs and bodies to get there.

As I gathered them in my arms that laughter sounded again, along with the slamming of doors and locks clicking in place. I had a feeling that these were locks I couldn't undo, and why would I want to? The Priscillas were dead.

Forty-Nine

I was vaguely aware of Zeid saying, "Shh, it will be all right," but I didn't believe him. In fact, the more that everyone tried to calm me, the madder I got. "How can you be so insensitive? What is the matter with all of you? We are locked in a room because Abbadon knows who we are, and the Priscillas are dead. It's over. We might as well be dead too."

"Stop it," Aki hissed. "Get a grip. You are not helping anything or anyone by acting crazy."

But I couldn't stop. I felt as if I had fallen down a well and was drowning. I was only vaguely aware of my surroundings. "Put her out for now," I heard Niko say. I had the briefest moment of terror and then nothing.

When I woke up, I was propped up against the wall. I couldn't see anything at all it was so dark. It hadn't been this dark before. The darkness added another layer to my anger and terror.

"She's awake," I heard someone say. It sounded like Pris, but that was impossible. The last thing I remembered was seeing the Priscillas lying dead in Niko's lap.

"Where am I? What's going on?"

This time it was Aki who answered me. "Are you calm, Kara?

We could actually use some of your clear questions right now."

A cold surrender came over me. Zut, why not. I'd ask questions. Maybe we would get out of here, maybe not. But at least I could do it for the Priscillas. Beru had taught me to use my anger. Now was the time to find it and destroy the monster that killed my friends.

"No. I'm not calm, I'm furious," was my answer. "And I'm ready to do what needs to be done."

"Don't scream, Kara. Actually, don't say anything," Aki said.

It was only when I felt Aki's hands on my eyes that I realized that I was blindfolded, and my hands were tied together. I wanted to scream then. Why blindfold me? Why tie my hands together. But I nodded my agreement.

Aki lifted the blindfold and untied my hands. I couldn't believe what I was looking at, and if Aki hadn't put her hand over my mouth, I might have screamed.

We were still in the room that we had been thrown into, but instead of being bound in the corner, Zeid and Niko were huddled with Pita and talking about something. That was surprising enough. How did Pita get here?

But that wasn't why Aki had her hand on my mouth. The Priscillas were sitting on Zeid's shoulder looking a little ragged, but perfectly okay.

I crawled over to the little group, and Pris came over and pulled my hair. "You should know better, Kara Beth."

I nodded numbly. How could I be so stupid?

I guess Pris took pity on me because she whispered in my ear, "We didn't have time to tell you, Kara. We had to get into the room so we let the Raiders think they captured us along with Niko and Zeid."

"But why did you look like you were dead?"

"They would have never let us live. Abbadon is afraid of

fairies, so Niko pretended to kill us because we betrayed him."

I was so embarrassed. "How did everyone else know and not me?"

"You didn't stop to think. Everyone else did."

There was really nothing else to say. It was true. I reacted.

Zeid looked over at me and smiled. That helped.

"Are you ready to get this done now, Kara?" Niko asked.

"I'm ready. But get what done?"

"It's time. We are going after Abbadon. We have a plan. And you are the key. Are you sure you are ready?"

I was never going to be sure, but I was ready, so I gave him the only answer I could, "Yes. I am."

******

It was Zeid who told me what happened. We were sitting against the wall holding hands, and I was finally calm enough to pay attention to the room. It was a horrible room to be in. Bodies were everywhere. Some of them were lying across each other. Most of them looked dead, and in various stages of decay. That wasn't the worst part though. It was the people that were alive, moaning and crying.

When I had asked how we were going to get out of the room, Niko told me we weren't. We were staying. It was part of the plan. Pita had left right after I woke up from the "sleep" that Aki had put me in.

He had barely looked at me. I know he was disappointed in my reaction, and I didn't blame him. I was too. However, even after I knew the Priscillas were okay, I still felt the wrench of pain that I had felt when I thought they had died. Just the memory made me feel like crying again.

It wasn't just the memory of what I thought had happened

to the Priscillas. It was what I had to do next. I had no idea how I was going to pull off the grand plan to destroy Abbadon, the real Abbadon, free the people he had captured, and then return home.

Actually, that last part I was pretty sure wasn't going to happen. Not for me. And I had to let it be okay. I had agreed to the plan, and I knew the risks.

"Tell me again what happened," I asked Zeid. I was sure I had missed details, and I needed them all if I was going to be successful.

Fifty

Zeid told me that he and Niko had done what Pita asked. Zeid had captured one of the mechanical waiters, and Niko had captured a Raider. Pita and Teddy had been waiting, and they took the two captives down into the tunnels with them.

But someone had seen what Zeid and Niko had done, and when they tried to return to the Raiders, they were captured and beaten as they tried to get them to tell what had happened to the other two men. Zeid and Niko kept shrugging as if they didn't know what they were talking about.

When one of the Raiders showed them a box with the three Priscillas in it, they both almost broke. But they caught a break. The Raiders told them that if they killed the fairies, they would believe them.

So Niko did. He did what Aki had done to me. But in the Priscillas' case, he made them look dead. After that, the Raiders were confused. Maybe these two weren't the men that Abbadon had told them to capture.

But just in case, they dragged them to the room we were in, and threw them in with the dead and dying.

"Well, they must have figured it out. Otherwise, we wouldn't be here," I said.

"They must have reported to Abbadon, and he told them who you were, and then sent them to get us."

"Not the same Raiders," Niko said, tilting his head towards a pile of what looked like dead Raiders.

"Those are the ones. He punished them for what we had done, and sent new ones to get you."

"If he knows who we are, then he must know who Anne is too. Why isn't she here?"

When Garth looked over at me with a look of terror, I knew that he was also asking that question. Where was his sister? Did Abbadon already kill her? If Niko and Zeid were correct about what was happening, then he wouldn't have, just as he hadn't killed any of us yet either.

It was perfectly obvious that he could have, at any time. We had been in his sights from the moment we arrived. Well, not every moment. We had evaded his Raiders more than once, but we had made it easy for him as we marched straight into his Castle thinking that was a wise thing to do.

Abbadon must have thought we were complete idiots, because he probably knew why we had come, risking our lives to do so, and he was toying with us as a cat plays with a mouse.

On the other hand, perhaps he didn't know that we weren't mice.

No, he wouldn't have killed Anne yet because he was using her as bait. The real Abbadon, not the one Anne thought she had fallen in love with and who had proposed to her.

Whoever that man was he wasn't Abbadon, because now we knew where the real Abbadon lived. We didn't know what he looked like, but we would know him when we saw him.

Pita had brought the news that gave us an advantage. He and Teddy had done a quick survey of the two men Zeid and Niko had captured. As we had guessed, the waiter was a very sophisticated version of the metal toadstools. They operated independently of a network, which was a disappointment because Pita and Teddy were hoping to trace the signal back to Abbadon but hadn't been able to do it with the waiter-robots.

The Raider was a different story. He was put into a room that blocked all signals from anywhere. He had food, water, and clean clothing. The room wasn't empty. It was beautiful. It had flowers, artificial light that felt like the sun, and a bathroom with a shower. And Teddy.

At first, the Raider had been angry, but he was no match for Teddy, who kept speaking to him as if he was a confused child while holding off his attempts at violence. The short version of the story was the Raider had collapsed, and when he woke, he was confused. The last thing he remembered was being captured.

So that had proved one of our theories. Abbadon was controlling the Raiders using a signal, which caused a form of hypnosis. And with that knowledge, we knew that once we stopped Abbadon, it might be possible to liberate the people, too.

Our other theory was that there was more than one man who looked like what we had thought was Abbadon. Whether they were real men changed to look the same, and controlled like the Raiders, or mechanical men, or clones, was something we didn't know yet.

What we did know was where the real Abbadon was, and that was our secret weapon. Pita and Teddy had traced the signal to the Raider and found the building where Abbadon lived.

At the moment it felt as if we had the upper hand. But, we didn't have long to act. Abbadon would have figured out where the two men had gone, and why.

Teddy and Pita had moved Tarla into a tunnel far away,

and they were the only ones left in the tunnels below us. It was dangerous for them to be there, but we needed them, and they knew it, so they stayed.

Before we stopped talking, I had asked the question again that we all had been asking all along. Why? Why was Abbadon doing this? What did he get out of killing everyone? What made him begin? What was the trigger?

One question we thought we knew the answer to and it was the one we were going to use against him. He wanted me. No, we didn't know why. Yes, I was the daughter of his brother, but so what? I wasn't even a powerful mage. My magic skills were middle of the road. I didn't feel as if I was that pretty. I wasn't that talented. Why me?

Perhaps we would find out soon. There was nothing to do but wait. Abbadon would send his Raiders to get us, and the games would really begin. It wouldn't be long before they came, and it wouldn't be long before this was over.

I hoped I would be strong enough to carry out the plan. No one had to remind me what was at stake. Nothing much. Just all life in Erda.

Fifty-One

We were all huddled together when they came for us. Niko had his arm around Aki. Zeid and I were still holding hands, the Priscillas were in my tunic pocket, and Garth sat on my other side. I was grateful for his presence and had my head on his shoulder. Not for me. For him. I couldn't imagine the anxiety he was going through wondering if his sister was okay.

When the door flew open, the Priscillas scrambled out of my pocket, and as we agreed, hid behind one of the bodies dumped in the corner. We figured that no one would look for them thinking that they were already dead.

The Raiders came straight towards us, kicking other bodies out of the way, keeping their vacant eyes on us at all times. They made that same noise we had heard before, grunting, mumbling, groaning. There were three for each one of us. They weren't taking any chances. I kicked and screamed as they dragged me out of the room. It wasn't all the act that we had agreed to. I was unbelievably terrified. But I was also prepared, and so was everyone else.

None of us used any of our skills to get away. If we used them, it was possible that we could escape, but for what? We could run back to the portal, and return home. But then, once again we would have failed, as we had learned that we had done in the past. None of us wanted ever to do this again. When, and if, we returned home, it would not be to a wasteland.

Besides, I knew there was a choice for me to make. But so far I hadn't been given one. Well, that wasn't entirely true. I was constantly given choices, but they were the same choices as everyone else.

This choice was going to be one that only I could make, and no one had a clue what it could be. We had to play our roles according to Abbadon's plans and hope that we were fooling him. We had a small advantage. He remembered our failing. He would be expecting us to fail again.

Nothing was said to us as the Raiders dragged us through the Castle, just more grunting and dead stares. During my first week in Erda, Beru had taught me how to feel where I was going so I wouldn't ever be lost. And that was what I was doing in the middle of all my kicking and screaming. That was the outside part of me. Inside I was paying attention to the doors we passed. It was still surprising to me that the Castle looked so much like the one in Zerenity. Looked like. Didn't feel like.

This Castle held no peace for anyone in it. Behind every door, I could feel the range of emotions from fear to sorrow, but there was nothing that suggested even the slightest happiness anywhere. It was a place of misery. It was a confirmation of what I had been thinking.

Back in the room waiting for the Raiders, I asked Aki if she thought Abbadon fed off of negative emotions. Was that the difference between Abbadon and his brother Darius?

Aki had nodded and agreed. Yes, that was what the man who looked like Abbadon had told her.

"So, Abbadon is like the serial killers in the Earth dimension? He gets his kicks from the pain of others?" I asked.

"If that's true," Garth said, "it would explain why he continues to escalate his reign of terror. He would need a bigger and bigger fix. Thinking ahead to when there was no one left to kill, would deny him what he needs now. More fear. More anger. More death."

Niko nodded. "It would answer many of our questions about why he is doing this. Perhaps there was a trigger, but once he began, he couldn't stop. It also makes sense because if your story about the bored brothers in the spaceship is true, that is what they intended isn't it? Good against evil. Light against dark.

"Which makes you wonder if those spaceship brothers themselves were good and evil, light versus dark. And if that was true, how did the two of them live together for so long? Wouldn't one of them have killed the other?"

Niko's question kept going through my head as we passed through the hallways. There was something in the question that contained the answer to how to stop Abbadon.

Although we had all stopped communicating mentally in case Abbadon could read our thoughts, we knew each other so well that when I saw Niko look over at me and nod, I figured he was thinking along the same lines.

Eventually, the Raiders pulled us into one of the buildings outside the Castle, opened the door, and threw us inside. I had expected another dungeon-like room, but instead, it was bright and sunny, with white filmy curtains blowing with the light breeze that was passing through the room. We stood there filthy and confused.

Aki whispered, "Abbadon is a tricky man. He keeps throwing us off base. Remember nothing is as it appears to be."

Aki's words burned inside of me, how could I have forgotten? Nothing is as it seems to be. I had to stop looking at everything as if it was real. And Aki was right, Abbadon was tricky because what came next was nothing like we expected.

Men and women who looked very much like our waiters appeared from around the corner. Beautiful people. The exact opposite of the frightening Raiders. I knew they weren't real, which made them even scarier. Abbadon would have made sure they could overpower anything we threw at them.

Once again, there were three of them for each of us. The men took Niko, Zeid, and Garth, and the women took Aki and me.

"Where are we going?" I asked, not expecting an answer.

But one of the women stopped and turned to me and said, "We need to clean and dress you for the wedding."

Terror swept over me. "Anne is marrying Abbadon?"

"No," she answered. "You are."

Fifty-Two

Someone screamed. It could have been me. Actually, I am pretty sure it was me. Not the response a man would want to hear from his prospective bride. As the women escorted me from the room, I heard Zeid yelling. I knew he wasn't acting as he screamed, "No, no, no!"

Instead of another dungeon-like room, the room that they took me to was beautiful. Or it would have been lovely if it wasn't in Abbadon's Keep. It was as if he read my mind and made a bedroom that looked like it belonged in the Earth Realm.

But I knew this wasn't a bedroom for me. It was a bedroom for a husband and wife. For Abbadon and me. And even though it was beautiful, the emotions and feeling swirling around the space were not of beauty but terror.

It was as if the negative feelings had been built into the walls. Instead of the scent of flowers and fresh air, anxiety and fear was the perfume that filled the space.

The women were gentle with me, and I wondered if they really were mechanical. Especially when one of the women looked at me, and for a moment her eyes weren't blank. They were engaged. When I looked again, they were back to the vacant stare that marked the mechanical beings rather than the manipulated ones. So I wondered if I was mistaken.

Instead of calling them mechanical people, I supposed that I could call them robots. But robots back in the Earth Realm didn't look like this. Perhaps they would someday. However, I knew that the metal toadstools that served us in my father's Castle had feelings. I'd heard them laugh, and shiver with pleasure when I patted them or thanked them for bringing my food, so even if they were human-made, to me, they were sentient beings.

Perhaps these women would be the same. As they drew a bath for me, I tried speaking with them. I asked them questions and received no answers. The more they ignored me, the more afraid I became. I was alone. I had no idea what was happening to my friends in the other rooms. Even though we had agreed not to speak with each other, I couldn't help myself. I reached out mentally to them. Anyone, please answer me. There was nothing. I was back to being ordinary. I had a terrible thought. Perhaps my magic was gone too. My team was gone. I was marrying Abbadon.

In spite of telling myself to be calm, I couldn't stop the feeling of terror that advanced over me like a cloud. I could almost see it enveloping me with a thick dark mass. I tried to stop it, but when it arrived, I was overwhelmed with fear. I struggled, and cried, and moaned a little in terror.

However, just before the cloud arrived, I withdrew a piece of myself into what I thought of as a safe room and became an observer. I watched myself struggle. I saw my fear and terror as if it was an object separate from me attempting to get into the safe room. And then I noticed a strange thing.

The more unhappy I got, the more terror or anger I felt, the more energy the women seemed to have. The thought occurred to me that I was feeding them. That idea fit into what we had discussed about Abbadon. That he fed off of negative emotions.

Maybe he designed his robots and Raiders to project those negative emotions and create more of them, collect them, and feed them back to him. Perhaps everything about the Castle and the Keep was designed to supply Abbadon. What would happen if he didn't get fed?

Here was a choice I could test. If I could become light-hearted and gay, and truly be happy for a moment, what would happen? I thought it would be impossible given how anxious I felt, but I was in a beautiful space, basking in a warm tub filled with bubbles. It was very incongruous. Just as Niko said, it was Abbadon confusing the mind, and making us wonder if he was a good man after all. Keeping us off balance.

But I could turn that against him, at least for a moment in this room. I could relax into the beauty, think about the love I felt for all of the people of Erda and my team. I could enjoy the hot water, the soap, the beautiful dress I could see laid out for me on the bed.

Yes, it was a wedding dress, but it was stunning. I focused on the good and the beautiful. I stopped screaming and starting saying, "thank you, thank you, thank you," over and over again. I looked at each woman and projected my gratitude for their care. At first, it was one of the hardest things I had ever done.

It was a battle, but it was all mine. I wasn't destroying anything. I was building up. As I looked at each woman in turn and thanked them, they became more and more agitated. Except for one. And at that moment I was sure she wasn't a robot at all. Her eyes changed from a vacant, detached look, to a pale blue and then dark blue and back to the vacant stare of the others.

But I knew who she was. I almost gave it away by saying her name out loud, but I stopped myself. I hid her identity by repeating my mantra of gratitude over and over again. I couldn't give her away. I didn't want Abbadon to read any of my thoughts except for the one proclaiming as loud and as often as I could, the beauty of creation.

Part of me was expecting what came next. If I thought the cloud of anxiety and fear was terrible before, the one that advanced on me faster than I thought possible was massive. I hid once again in my safe room, and let the rest of me react to the fear thrown on me and the women in the room. We were being punished.

But I had learned something that could be a weapon, and Aki's mother, Tarla, was on our side and knew what we had to do. She had told me so in that one split second before the cloud arrived.

I clutched that hope tight to my heart as the rest of the world turned dark.

Fifty-Three

After all the screaming stopped, I was exhausted. To be clear, it was me screaming. Screaming out of fear, because the cloud that arrived showed me all my friends being tortured, and a menacing voice kept saying over and over again, "This is all your fault."

I had been put into bed, probably by the women, and as I lay there, I reminded myself that negative emotions were temptations that when indulged would take me away from my true self. Not that I knew precisely what that true self meant, or was, but I knew for sure it wasn't what Abbadon was promoting. As I thought about the feelings of guilt that threatened to overcome me, I knew that it was a negative emotion that was feeding the monster. It wasn't helping me at all.

Plus, how did I know those pictures were real? "Nothing is as it seems." That's what Aki had reminded me. Nothing. I touched the necklace and bracelet that I still wore. I wondered why I had been allowed to keep them. Perhaps Abbadon didn't know that they were magic? Then a thought occurred to me. What if he couldn't see them? That idea was so wonderful, I almost popped into happiness, but I restrained myself.

I didn't want to give anything away. I had an idea of how to defeat Abbadon, and now that I practiced on the women, and saw what happened, I was pretty sure it would work. It could backfire on us though. If Abbadon reacted that strongly against the small amount of good that I had projected, what would he do if we all did it?

And how was I going to tell everyone about what I had discovered? Keeping the outward expression of anxiety and fear intact, I allowed myself to wonder if the Priscillas had managed to escape and do what we had asked them to do.

I rolled over in bed wondering when and who would come to get me for the wedding, and heard a muffled, "Ouch!" It was hard to keep from squealing in pleasure, but keeping emotions neutral, I lifted the covers and saw all three Priscillas, lounging there, looking as beautiful as always. Pris' hair was a little untidy, probably from the sheets being over her, but their eyes were bright and shining. They were the most beautiful things I had ever seen.

"We saw, and felt what you did, Kara Beth," Pris whispered. "And we told everyone else."

"Are they fine?" I asked, even though I was a little afraid to find out.

"Everyone is fine. In fact, more than fine. Like you, they have been cleaned, fed, and rested."

The Priscillas and I didn't need to say out loud what we were thinking. Abbadon was doing this to put them off guard. Make them more confused. Wonder if he was the monster that they knew him to be after all.

Cil nodded, knowing what I was thinking. "We think that at the wedding he will begin to torture them. It will work for him by getting you to say yes, but also to feed what he needs to be happy. But we are ready, and so is the rest of the team."

"And the portal?" I asked.

"Garth says it will be ready."

"But what about Anne?" I hadn't seen her since dinner the night before. How did she feel about me marrying Abbadon? Was she safe?

La gave me the answer. "Anne is fine too. She is being prepped to be your maid of honor."

The four of us stared at each other. That meant she would be the target of Abbadon's greatest torture.

As the Priscillas prepared to leave, I asked them the question that was tearing me apart inside.

"What do I say? Yes or no?"

They shook their heads, and Cil said, "No one knows the answer. Did you say yes before, or no before? No one remembers. No one knows. This one is all yours, Kara Beth."

Then the Priscillas did what I had seen Aki, Zeid, and even Leif and Sarah do, but I had never seen the Priscillas do. They vanished. It took my breath away. Had they always been able to do that? Would I ever have a chance to learn? Tears started rolling down my face.

I was afraid that I was heading towards my old stomping grounds, the pit of self-pity, when La returned for a second and whispered in my ear, "Aki says that you will know, and you are not alone," and then she was gone again.

This time I didn't hold back my sobs. Let Abbadon feed on them. He would think they were tears of fear, but they weren't. They were tears of remembering the first time Aki had said those words to me.

I was new to Erda. I thought I was alone then too. But since then I had discovered the people that would always stand with me, as I would stand with them. Those words were true for everyone. We were never alone. All we had to do was reach out, accept, and receive the help always available.

I only knew one person who was alone, and it was going to be his undoing. Abbadon.

In the middle of my crying fit, the door opened and a group of women stepped into the room. They looked like the same women, but I couldn't be sure, and I knew that Tarla couldn't take the chance of showing herself to me again.

"Time to get dressed," one of the women said. I was helped out of bed and led to a dressing table. With a mirror. Of course, mirrors wouldn't be banned here. It was Abbadon who saw through them. Mirrors were another way he would be watching over me.

I hadn't seen myself in a mirror for over a year, not since the trip through a portal that transformed me from a twelve-year-old to a woman. I had only imagined what I must look like.

The woman who stared back at me was familiar. I supposed I had seen myself before. Before mirrors were banned from the Kingdom of Zerenity.

As I stared, I realized my eyes were too calm. I was too calm. I had to project more anxiety and fear. As I transformed my outward expression, I caught a glimpse of one of the women who gave me an almost imperceptible nod. Tarla. She knew what I knew.

Things were not as they seemed, and I was never alone. This I knew, and it was knowledge I was hiding until I could use it as a weapon. But first, I had a choice to make. What would it be? It would mean the difference between failing everyone in Erda or saving them.

I used to think that I had hard decisions to make. After this one, everything would be easy.

Yes or no. Which would it be?

Fifty-Four

The women took the wedding dress from the bed and helped me into it. It felt as beautiful on as it looked. Surprising me. I expected to feel miserable, but instead, I felt beautiful. More disorientation from Abbadon. The woman I knew was Tarla guided me to stand in front of the mirror.

I stood there transfixed by what I saw. A young woman who could be a Queen stood before me. Is that what Abbadon wanted? A queen to his king? Why not Anne then? Was it really Abbadon who had asked Anne to marry him?

There was always the possibility that it was me that Abbadon wanted to marry because I was supposed to become the Queen of the Kingdom of Zerenity. By marrying me, he would rule all of Erda.

Besides, my marrying the monster who had killed so many people, including my mother, would devastate my father. Would devastate all of Zerenity. Abbadon could feast on those feelings for a long time.

I would be a traitor to my people. Or at least that would be what they thought. But what if by marrying him I saved my people? Did it matter what they thought as long as I saved them?

Tarla fit the veil onto my head. A traditional wedding. How odd. And not. Again, Abbadon was using all that we treasured against us. Zeid would see me walking down the aisle ready to marry a monster. His heart would break, as would mine. But if it would save Erda, I would say yes. If only I knew what the answer should be.

I longed for a voice in my head to tell me which to choose. But I had already been warned that it was my choice, and it was only my choice that would work. What had I chosen before? If I could remember, it would be so easy.

There was a knock on the door, and six young men entered—the same kind of young men who had waited on us our first night in Abbadon's Castle. Two stood beside me, two walked in front of me, and two behind as we left the room and headed down the hallway.

It could have been almost pleasant, except that the hall was lined with Raiders, mumbling, snorting, and grunting as we passed. It was the perfect reminder of where we were, and what would happen if I said the wrong thing.

I stumbled. Still clumsy. Fear was making it worse. The young man on my right caught my arm before I fell. I jerked away, unwilling to be touched, and glared at him. His vacant, expressionless eyes, briefly flashed light blue, and then it was gone. Not a robot. I knew who it was. It was Niko.

Using every ounce of my self-control, I kept fear in place. Fear and nausea. I let the anxiety flood over me and pushed that emotion out into the hallway as we walked. Maybe I couldn't use magic here, but I could use negative emotions since that was what Abbadon needed. That I could give him.

Hidden inside that private room inside myself, another flame of hope ignited. Tarla walked behind me holding the train of my dress, Niko walked beside me. The Priscillas were somewhere in the Castle doing whatever they were planning. If I gave the right answer, it was possible we could defeat Abbadon.

I let the worry of what would happen to my friends play out as terror that Abbadon could feel. I let the hope that all my friends were safe sustain me. Niko was beside me. Perhaps they were free too.

My hope didn't last long.

****

The guards led us to what looked like a traditional church back home in the Earth Realm. *You've got to be kidding*, I thought to myself.

It was glorious. It had all the turrets and stained glass windows found in the magnificent cathedrals in Europe. That beauty made the whole thing worse. Abbadon was copying an Earth tradition that meant something and turning it into a farce.

I thought that perhaps some of the beings he had captured during the last few centuries had been used to build it. I wondered how many lives were lost constructing it. As we stepped into the narthex of the cathedral, the difference became apparent.

Although I had never visited the Notre Dame Cathedral, I had heard people talk about it. They always said they would go back over and over again to experience it. It wasn't just the fact that it was stunning; it was what it felt like inside. Enveloped by love. Inspired. Hopeful. It had filled them with the awareness of connection, of the Oneness of everything.

Not this cathedral. Yes, it was physically stunning. But the experience inside was cold and heartless. The fear and sorrow of those who had built it seeped out of its walls. The misery that Abbadon lived with was in every cell of the building. It was physically painful to stand there. Because I knew it pleased Abbadon, I let myself feel that pain and I amplified it to send it back to him. I hoped that would be enough for him, the fact that I was willing to suffer so he could be happy.

But when the doors of the church opened to reveal the long walk to the altar, I knew it wouldn't be. Standing beside the last few pews were two Raiders, and placed between them were Zeid, Garth, and Aki. Dressed for a wedding.

There was no doubt in my mind, they were there to be tortured, and since everyone was there but Niko, it would be worse. Abbadon knew that Niko had escaped.

I prayed that he didn't realize that Niko walked beside me.

Fifty-Five

Anne stood at the front of the church, waiting for me. My maid of honor. Her red hair was piled elegantly on the top of her head, and the rose-colored bridesmaid dress that she wore was perfect for her. She was lovely. There was no sign of Abbadon. She stood there alone, looking radiant in spite of all that was going on. Inwardly, I breathed a sigh of relief. She was still safe.

There was no sound anywhere inside the church. Not even the breath of the guards that stood beside me could be heard. Then, without warning the silence was replaced with organ music blasting off the walls. It was so loud that without thinking everyone put their hands to their ears, and cringed. Within seconds it was turned down. I was sure someone would be punished for that mistake.

As traditional wedding music played, I stood in the back of the church wondering who was going to walk me down the aisle or was I supposed to walk by myself. Suddenly the Raiders guarding Zeid pushed him forward. He stumbled. They pulled him up and brought him to the back of the church where I waited for my signal to walk forward.

It was obvious. Zeid would walk me down the aisle. Then he

was to hand his future bride, the one that was supposed to be his destiny, over to another man. Not a man. A monster.

It was brilliant planning on Abbadon's part. More pain. The perfect torture for both of us. And I would give Abbadon that. I would give him all the pain I could find inside myself, and I knew that Zeid was doing the same thing.

We were feeding him. I hooked my hand onto Zeid's arm, and we began the slow walk down the aisle towards the empty space where my groom should have been waiting.

When would he show himself? For our plan to work, he had to be present. The more pain and terror and sorrow we fed him, the more we hoped he would reveal himself to suck up more. The walls were ringing with terror. It was so bad I had trouble walking. If Zeid hadn't been holding me up, my knees would have buckled, and I would have fallen.

But together we walked. The music played. We took those shuffle-down-the aisle little steps, and then smaller ones, letting our fear build. We tapped into the fear of the Raiders. We pulled the horror that was built into the cathedral out of the ceiling where it had been trapped, and attached it to the sound of the organ.

Fear and terror wove through the cathedral, making it harder and harder to function, and still, Abbadon did not appear. Finally, I realized what he was waiting for. He wanted my choice now. Before he showed himself.

And now I knew what it had to be. It had to be yes. Zeid glanced at me and then looked away. Yes, he was telling me, it has to be yes. And you have to mean it. For all the wrong reasons, because that is what he wants. He wants a bride steeped in terror. He wants to control her. He wants to win with evil.

So I said, "Yes. Yes, Abbadon, I will marry you." And I meant it. I would marry him. I would stay in his Castle and live a life filled with pain and terror. It was the only way.

As we got closer to the altar, I could see Anne's eyes brimming over with her own pain. Pain for me, pain for herself and for the man she thought she had loved.

I knew the Priscillas had somehow gotten to her and told her the plan because for the briefest of seconds she smiled and then pushed out her pain. It was like a tsunami of pain pushing out into the church, washing over everyone, grabbing them into the undertow.

Zeid and I matched it. I could feel Aki and Garth doing the same. Only the robot men and women walking beside me stayed neutral. That included Tarla and Niko. They couldn't let the slightest whisper of emotion give them away.

Five feet away and still no groom. I yelled so loud that I knew it could be heard outside if anyone was listening. Yelled it with my entire being. "Yes. Yes. Yes, I will marry you, Abbadon."

It was our last hope. I meant it. I let him see that I meant it.

And then the purple curtain behind the altar opened, and two men walked out.

One was a man who looked like Abbadon, and one was a man we had never seen before, dressed as a priest. Ready to marry us.

The two of them walked towards the front of the altar. The priest stood behind Anne and Abbadon, arms hidden inside the sleeves of his robe, his face a mask.

Abbadon smiled at me, and I saw the sadness in his eyes. How could Abbadon be sad? Everything we knew about Abbadon told us he could not experience sadness. Were we wrong about what he wanted and who he was? Or was the man waiting to marry me not Abbadon?

We had to know. It was time. I reached up and pushed the blue star hanging around my neck. The 4D version of the world appeared in front of me.

There was so much more to see than what we could see with 3D vision. The strands of terror and fear that we felt were visible. Energy throbbed from the Raiders, and I could see the constraints that held them captive.

In spite of where we were, there was beauty behind all the fear Abbadon was producing and feeding on.

And I saw what we were looking for. I saw the true being called Abbadon, and I knew that the weapon we had in reserve could be used to defeat him. If we used it correctly.

In the meantime, I had to project doubt and fear, but inside I had more than hope. I had the knowledge that it could work.

Fifty-Six

I remembered the first time Beru told me about Abbadon. She said that no one was sure what Abbadon looked like, and if they had seen him, they didn't live long. I prayed that was true. I hoped that I wouldn't live long with him, but I would live as long as possible to save everyone I loved.

Before I let go of Zeid's arm to go to my future husband, I whispered that I loved him. Perhaps we would find each other again in another lifetime. Zeid was doing everything that he could to not keep me from leaving him. His heart was breaking, and he allowed that pain to feed Abbadon too. He did it for me. He was letting me go to save Erda. He would return, and someday he would be King, but without me by his side.

But first, we had to free the people that Abbadon had captured. We knew that Abbadon would not let them go. He would use them to produce the pain and terror he needed to survive. However, I knew how to stop him. I knew how to keep him from continuing to destroy Erda, but to do that I had to stay and be his wife.

We didn't try to hide how terrible it was for us to part. I backed away from Zeid holding his hand and looking deeply into his eyes so I would have that memory with me as I lived in

Abbadon's Castle. Then I turned and walked to my husband, Abbadon.

And as I walked, I turned on the weapon we had kept in reserve, the one that would free Abbadon's people and make me his prisoner. I passed the man we called Abbadon and walked up to the man disguised as a priest. Standing inches away from his face, a face that hid what I knew to be something other than a man, and said, "I love you Abbadon. I accept you as my husband." I pulled every ounce of love I had ever felt out of my body and projected it onto him. He began to tremble.

Then from every corner, every stone, every crack in the Cathedral love vibrated forth, projected by Niko, Aki, Anne, Garth, Tarla, and Zeid. It swept through the church destroying every fiber of evil that had thrived there.

Abbadon stared at me as I held his eyes, giving him love, calling him husband. By now his hands had escaped his robes, and I caught them, pulling him closer, whispering that I loved him. I had to mean it.

The next wave of love slammed into him, as Ruta and his trees sent love across his Kingdom. The Priscillas had enlisted all their insect friends, and they too sent out love.

Beneath our feet, every Ginete and Whistle Pig that Pita and Teddy could find sent waves of love through the earth. The ground trembled beneath our feet.

Behind me, I could hear the Raiders moan and then in their own voices cry out in joy. Somehow they understood what we were doing, and many of them pushed past their anger at what he had done to them and joined in the sending out of waves, and waves, of love.

Outside the Castle, thunder cracked, and slashes of lightning flashed down into the earth. Rain began to pelt the land. I knew it was pushing the tendrils of evil down to the ground where they would continue until they were purified.

While we held the being we knew as Abbadon captured in the web of unrelenting, unbiased, and unconditional love he was powerless, so Niko opened our channel. It was heaven to hear everyone's voice in my head again. I would miss those voices when they were gone.

"It's time for you to leave," I said. "Anne is the portal open?"

Out of the corner of my eye, I could see Anne leaning into the man we had thought to be Abbadon. He had his arms around her, sobbing. He was free.

"I am staying here, too," Anne said. "But I'm opening the portal for you. It's okay. Our past selves went to the future, and so there will be more years for the future to know me."

Garth stepped to his sister and put his arm around her too. "I am staying too with you Anne."

More love swelled into the cathedral, and the being we called Abbadon remained captured in its beam.

"Go now," Anne said.

Behind me, I knew Tarla was hugging her grown children goodbye.

"Zeid, you will be a great King. Now take these people and go home," I said in my most queenly command voice. Because now I was Queen of Abbadon's Kingdom, and it was the greatest gift I could give to Zeid. My love and his freedom.

With our channel open, I could say goodbye to everyone, even those not in the church with us.

"Goodbye Ruta, thank you for being my great friend. Take care of Beru for me."

To Teddy, I said, "I love you forever Teddy Bear, will you make sure the Priscillas are safe with you back home?"

Hooking my arm into Abbadon's, I turned to face my friends in the church one last time. I let the love I felt for them, and all of the ones I loved back in the future Zerenity, flow out and encase my new husband and me.

Now that he was in this weakened state, I could hold him in that bubble of love for the rest of his life. I would use the love I felt for Zeid, and the team that had taught me so much, to fuel that love. I knew it would never run out.

Although none of us knew how what we had done in this timeline would affect our future, I had to hold onto the hope that everyone would return safely and find a restored Erda. Maybe even the people who had died would have returned, and Ruta would find his mother. And maybe mine.

The vision of my father and mother reuniting fueled my love again.

I turned to the man we had thought to be Abbadon. His eyes were filled with tears, and he said, "Thank you for releasing me. I am in your debt forever."

I shook my head. "It wasn't me. It was all of us. All I ask is that you make Anne happy."

He bowed and said, "That is an easy promise to keep."

Within minutes the five of us were alone in the church. The channel was closed again. I knew it was because the team had made it to the portal and were no longer in the past with us. Abbadon was caught in the web of love we had woven for him. It was time for us to begin our new life. A life lived in the past so that we could protect the future.

Fifty-Seven

As the five of us started walking down the aisle of the cathedral, I was strangely happy. I had fulfilled my destiny. Zeid was fulfilling his. The little girl Hannah who had such big dreams in the Earth dimension, and then discovered that she was a princess in another one, had grown up.

I had never wanted to be a Queen, but I had accepted that future. Not Queen of Zerenity but the Queen of Abbadon's Kingdom. Dreams of what I could do flooded through me. Now that love had released everyone from Abbadon's grip it could be beautiful. I hoped that the love I felt for that future would soften the sorrow I felt for no longer being with my friends that I loved more than life itself.

"That's obvious, because you gave up the life you dreamed of having for them," Anne said.

I had forgotten that Anne and Garth could also read my mind.

"You stayed, too."

"I stayed because I love this man. And Garth stayed because he loves me. Besides, now he can find that girl that he loved before. So we stayed for love, but not the love you have to give."

Still holding Abbadon's hand, I hugged all three of them,

thinking that it would be bearable because they were there.

"Thank you for staying here with me," I said.

"And me!" said a tiny voice. The same words I had heard once before when the speaker peeked out of my pocket a few days after I first returned to Erda.

Flying down the aisle straight at my hair was Pris, trailed by Cil and La.

Although I was overjoyed at seeing them, I whispered, "No, you were supposed to go home."

As Pris pulled at my hair, and Cil and La wiped the tears off my face, La answered for the three of them.

"We are home. You are our home."

There was so much love circling us that I wasn't afraid of letting go of Abbadon's hand. I patted his hand so he would know that I loved him too, and I gathered my three friends in my arms smothering them with kisses. "You weren't supposed to stay, but now that you are here, I am so happy."

As I spoke those words, a massive boom shook the cathedral. And then another. All of us clutched each other to stay upright. We had Abbadon in the middle of our circle, keeping him up. Even I was amazed that we had all moved to protect him. Love had healed our hearts too.

Another huge boom, a flash of light, and then a voice.

"You lost, brother."

A column of light shot through the ceiling to the floor in front of us. Abbadon began to tremble even more.

Inside the beam, I could see something move. The voice came from the light.

"You lost, brother. And look what your choice did to you. It turned you into a monster. You chose evil. You bet that evil would win. And yet, look at you now. Protected by people who should hate you, and yet they have defeated you with love. You lost, and now it is time to return."

"No, no," Abbadon said, his voice so weak it was hard to hear him. "I can't go back. I will be punished."

"Have you not learned anything?" the light asked, throwing out sparks that lit every corner of the church.

"Love defeated you. Do you think we would give up the power of love to punish you? Then we will have chosen the dark side as you did. No, you will punish yourself until you let go of your evil ways."

The being inside the light turned to face us as we held onto Abbadon. Softening its voice, it said, "Thank you. But you have to let him go now. We'll take care of him."

The light moved over all of us, and I could feel my grip on Abbadon loosening. Within a few seconds, Abbadon and the column of light disappeared.

It was over.

I felt empty and elated at the same time. I was free! Abbadon was gone. I was no longer his wife. Happiness should have been flooding over me, but instead, I started to cry. I wanted to be brave, but Anne knew what was bothering me.

"I'm sorry, Kara Beth. Now you are free, but you are here in the past. And we can't open the time portal for you. We were careful to lock it on the other side, just in case something went wrong."

I nodded, holding my head up, dashing the tears off my face. I had given up that life. I would have to find a new one here, in the past.

"Perhaps I can help you with that," said a voice from the back of the church. The church doors had remained open after everyone had gone, and now an old man stood in the entrance. As he walked forward to us, I went to meet him.

I remembered the old man that Aki and Niko had told us

about. "Are you the man who helped my friends Aki and Niko escape Abbadon?"

"That I am," the old man said.

I reached out and gathered him into my arms. "Thank you," I said.

The Priscillas started to laugh, and I turned to them, wondering what could be so funny. Pris just kept giggling, and even my sternest look didn't stop her.

"What's up with you?" I said.

"Oh Kara Beth, in spite of all the things you just did, you are still dense. Don't you know who that is?"

As I said, "No," I turned to look again and then felt like a complete idiot. Actually, it felt kinda good being an idiot again. No longer the person who had to hold a monster in the grip of love, I was just an ordinary girl, a little clumsy and a bit dense.

Standing in front of me was my friend from Earth and Erda. Leif stood there with a smile on his beautiful face, holding his favorite staff.

"Would you like to go home with me? Sarah is probably missing me."

I cried again, this time with tears of happiness. "Are you taking all of us?"

"No," Anne said, looking at her brother.

"We still want to stay here. We love it here. We'll take care of the past so you can return to a beautiful future."

We hugged one last time. I couldn't wait to see their future selves again. I wondered what they would remember.

The Priscillas had already attached themselves to my dress assuring me that they were coming with me. I touched Leif's shoulder as he raised his staff, tapped it on the floor, a blue haze rose around us, and then we were gone.

Fifty-Eight

If I had time to think before the blue haze swept us away, I would have thought we would return to the portal outside the Castle. But I was wrong. When the haze cleared, we were in the woods somewhere. For all I knew we hadn't traveled in time at all because the woods looked the same as any other woods.

I still had on my wedding dress which didn't quite fit into a woods venue. Leif was standing a few feet away. He appeared to be knocking on the air. He looked over his shoulder, eyes twinkling, and continued to knock. Perhaps I had gone crazy?

A few seconds later Sarah's head popped out of nowhere right where Leif had been knocking.

"Oh you are here!" she said, stepping into Leif's arms. Now I could see all of her and behind her was a slit in the air revealing what looked like a room of some kind.

Yes, I was going crazy. I couldn't move. Frozen in place, I began to think I had dreamed the whole thing. That is until I felt Sarah's arms around me holding me tight and whispering, "Welcome home, Kara Beth."

Seeing my puzzled face, Sarah said, "Look in 4D. Do it without the necklace."

Although I had struggled with 4D sight on my own before,

and expected to find it hard to do, within seconds of trying, my sight switched over, and I saw the cabin that just moments before was invisible to me.

"Oh!" was my brilliant response.

Once I saw the cabin, I didn't need to keep my 4D sight in place to continue to see it. The Priscillas and I followed Leif and Sarah inside, and I sighed in relief and happiness.

I felt welcomed. So different than Abbadon's Castle. Comfortable chairs and couches were arranged for conversation. Light streamed in from the windows that circled the room. All I wanted to do was sit in a chair and never move again. But Sarah took me by the hand and led me down the hall to a room with a big bed, with my favorite clothing lying on it.

Until that moment I hadn't realized how much I wanted to take off the dress that belonged in the past. "Get cleaned up, Kara," Sarah said. "And then we have one last thing to do before you can return to your future."

Although Sarah was smiling when she said those words, I felt a chill run down my spine. Weren't we done yet?

Although my body wanted me to take my time in the shower, my mind wouldn't let me. What had we missed? I dressed and hurried back to the small living and dining room. The table was set for tea, and the Priscillas were already sitting on it eating something that looked like a flower sandwich.

Through the windows, I could see Leif. He appeared to be carrying on a conversation with someone, but there was no one there but trees.

Sarah flicked her wrist, and I saw a light land on Leif's shoulder, and before I could blink, he was sitting at the table with us. Interesting way to get someone's attention, I'd have to learn that trick.

"Are you full of questions again, Kara?" Leif asked.

"Yes. Shall I ask them or could you just answer them because you must know what they are."

The Priscillas tittered, holding their hands over their mouth. I think they were afraid that I was being impertinent to a wizard, and I suppose that I was, but all I wanted was to go home. And the home I meant was back to my friends, and Zeid. It worried me that Zeid still thought that I was lost to him forever.

Sarah put her hand on Leif's arm as she addressed me. "No need to keep you waiting, Kara. You're right. No one knows you have returned. After all, it's only been a few hours, and they are all back at the Castle mourning and celebrating. Mourning for you, and celebrating the monster's evil has never touched the Erda they returned to."

"However, there is one place that has not been restored, and I think it would be important to you to do so before you return to the Castle.

"It's a task that only you can do. And to do it, we have to send you back in time once again."

My heart sank. Every cell of my body protested. I wanted to stay here. But at the same time, I knew that Sarah and Leif knew that I would do it. Whatever it was.

"Where am I going?"

"Back to a village that was destroyed before you returned to Erda. Not by the Shrieks, or Shatterskin, but by the monster we were calling Abbadon. It was personal to him, so he did it himself. And then he locked the destruction in place so it could never be undone."

"If it can never be undone, then what good would I do to go back to whatever village you are talking about?"

"Because he made one mistake. He didn't know that your mother had left the bracelet for you. That bracelet and your magic can stop him from locking it."

All the blood rushed out of my head, and I thought I was going to faint. "Are you talking about Ruta's village and my mother?"

Sarah and Leif nodded. "You mean I have to defeat Abbadon one more time, even though he is gone? Me? I have enough magic to do this? And if I don't, the village and everyone in it will remain destroyed?"

"That about sums it up. Except you have to go alone," Leif said, smiling at me as if he was merely asking me to go to the store for cream for his coffee.

The Priscillas looked on in disbelief. I felt as if the universe had slapped me. We did all that, and still one more thing to do. Not a small thing. Something more important than me. Again.

At that moment I understood. I had thought that my choice to marry Abbadon was the pivot choice. And perhaps it was, but this one, this one, was the one that determined my future, and who knows, maybe more than mine. Without all my magic, without my confidence in myself, I could not be Queen, and Erda could not thrive.

"Two questions. When do I go, and what do I need to know?"

Fifty-Nine

In the end, I didn't learn much from Leif or Sarah. All I knew was that I would arrive at the village right before Abbadon. I had to stop him from locking in the destruction. Since I didn't know how he locked it in, it seemed to me I had to stop him from doing it in the first place. Not that I knew how to do that either.

However, Leif and Sarah both assured me that I had everything I needed to accomplish the task. Still, I kept thinking they were leaving something out. Why would they do that? They wanted me to succeed. So why not tell me everything that I needed to know?

All I did know was that I was at the edge of a forest that bordered the path that Abbadon would be walking as he headed to the village to destroy it. Right before he encased me in the blue haze, Leif said, "Remember the bracelet."

I figured whatever was happening was why my mother left me the bracelet in the first place. I knew what I had done with it before. I had used it to magnify waves of energy. I had learned how to control the power so as not to kill, only stun.

Neither Sarah nor Leif seemed worried about sending me back to this time, so that meant I already knew what to do. At least that's what I told myself.

As I waited, it occurred to me that perhaps this was a test of my willingness to become who I was meant to be. I was thinking so deeply about that possibility, that I almost missed the signs that someone was coming. Someone that the creatures of the forest did not like. Everything had become silent. I could feel the beings of the woods moving away from the road and deeper into the woods.

It had to be Abbadon. I wondered if he would look like the monster I had seen or the man Abbadon pretended to be.

There was no point in confronting him head-on. I couldn't battle someone like Abbadon on my own. And Sarah and Leif knew it. What did I know that could stop Abbadon?

In a flash, it came back to me. I could use his own trick of illusion. If I could produce a strong enough field to protect the village from destruction, and then feed back to him the illusion that he had done it, then he would never know he had failed. I didn't have to defeat him using force. All I had to do was give him the illusion of success.

It would work. The question was, did I have enough magic to do so?

A blue haze flashed, and Leif stood beside me.

"You only had to choose, Kara. Now that you have figured it out, we can do this together."

****

What happened next would be burned into my memory for the rest of my life. Everything that Abbadon threw at the village, we reflected back to him as if it was happening.

That meant we had to spend time in his head hearing his thoughts and intentions. It was like entering a dark cave filled with creepy crawly things, terrible noises, and disgusting smells. We had to stay there to see what he expected to see so that we could produce it for him.

It was horrifying to be inside his thoughts and see the joy he was receiving by causing chaos and destruction. It was also terrifying because we couldn't let him know that we were there. Otherwise, the plan would fail and he would turn all his destruction on us, and I wasn't sure we could hold him off.

Abbadon had arrived looking like a man. That made it even worse. Anyone meeting him on the road would not know what he was. Not only had he disguised himself as a gentle and kind man, but he had also disguised his thinking to match.

The only thing that gave him away to us is that we had met him before. And of course, the creatures in the woods weren't fooled.

He had stationed himself where he could see the entire village and then let go with a destructive force so intense, Leif and I had to do everything we could to keep it from reaching the town. It was horrifying to witness the fierce pleasure Abbadon had as he destroyed.

What the encounter with Abbadon did for me was remove any illusion I had harbored that no one really meant to do harm. If I had an inkling of doubt that there were monsters I didn't have one after that. I knew it would make me a better Queen. I would not be easily fooled by charm or false kindness.

After it was all over and Abbadon had returned to his part of Erda thinking he destroyed the village, Leif had brought us both back to the cabin where Sarah and the Priscillas waited. I didn't waste time before asking them the obvious question.

"You sent me there to test me, didn't you?"

"Not so much to test you, but to teach you an invaluable lesson," Sarah replied. "And, it had to be you. No one else could have done it."

She was right. It was invaluable. I still knew that good was more powerful than evil, but I also had to recognize that evil is intentional, and to destroy it before it becomes as powerful as Abbadon had become. And I had to accept that it had to be me. I had to accept my destiny.

I was definitely not the twelve-year-old Hannah who had tripped over her own feet as she stepped out of the portal from Earth to Erda. I thought back to what Suzanne had told me then. That I had to become beautifully terrifying. Now I understood more of what she meant.

I could feel the strength of my magic, but more than that, I could feel the power of love that had defeated evil. Not me alone. All of us, the community, the Kingdom, my friends.

However, I was still curious, and I had a ton of questions.

"Would you like to wait to ask all those questions until after we return to the Castle?" Sarah asked, putting her arm around me.

Up until that moment I had not allowed myself to think about my friends. A part of me was afraid I would never be able to return. I was so overcome with gratitude I could only nod, "yes."

Sixty

After affirming with Leif and Sarah that everyone was safe back at the Castle, but not expecting me, I asked Leif and Sarah if we could arrive outside the Castle and walk to it. I wanted time to absorb what had happened before I was caught up in the celebration of my return.

Once again, nothing would be the same, and this time I wanted to face it head on, on my own terms. Besides, some of the questions I had didn't need to be answered in front of everyone.

They had agreed, and I think they were even a little pleased with my choice. Perhaps I was demonstrating some wisdom. And when Sarah suggested we wait until I had gotten a good night's sleep I was only too happy to say yes. In fact, I'm not sure I said anything at all because I didn't remember anything about going to bed.

The waking up was wonderful though. Pris, Cil, and La were sitting on my bed waiting for me. That was different. Pris was usually prying my eyes open if I slept in. I smiled at the three of them and lifted the covers. They didn't need to be invited twice. They snuggled under the covers with me and in a flash, I fell asleep again. Not before I thought I heard Pris snore. I suppressed a giggle. I had something to tease her about now.

I woke up again, this time to the smell of coffee and cinnamon buns. Sitting at the table with Leif, Sarah, and the Priscillas I felt as if I had been transported to heaven. I lingered over breakfast as long as I could. I hoped I could come to revisit this cabin someday. It was almost like being back in Earth. Another home for me, here in Erda.

"Of course, dear one," Sarah said. "You are welcome anytime. But perhaps it's time for us to go to the Castle, and give your friends the gift of your return?"

I had already dressed in the clothes that had been laid out for me, and the Priscillas had tucked themselves into my pocket. I smiled and started to say, "Yes," when I found myself on the road that led to the Castle. The other way led to Dalry. I couldn't wait to visit there again to see how it had fared in the future, but that visit would have to wait.

"How do you do that?" I asked Sarah and Leif. "And that is one of my first questions. If you could go back in time like that, why did we need the portal?"

"I used a different kind of portal, Kara Beth, and I could only take you through it. And only after you made that first choice," Leif answered.

"The choice to marry Abbadon?"

"The choice to do what had to be done for something bigger than yourself, and to do it with love in your heart, and not hate, resentment, or discouragement. Not an easy task, but you did it, Kara Beth. And look at what happened."

"But, it wouldn't have worked if I hadn't done it that way, or expected to be freed from the decision?"

Sarah looked at me with pride in her eyes. She didn't need to say anything. I felt the answer.

As we walked, I allowed myself to be back to the future. It's another reason that I chose to walk. I wanted to see the sky, feel the trees, and be at peace in this new self that I had acquired. I needed to be ready to face what I found at the Castle without breaking down.

Which meant there were more questions that I needed to ask before we got back. The first one was about the village.

"Since we stopped Abbadon from destroying Ruta's village then it never happened, right?"

Leif and Sarah nodded, and the Priscillas hopped up to my shoulders waiting for my next question.

"That means that Ruta's family and my mother never died? And if that is true, and you knew that, how did you keep it a secret from all of us, and why?"

"I think the why of it is obvious. If Abbadon knew he hadn't been successful at destroying the village he would have returned, and we would have to continue to play that time loop over and over again," Sarah answered.

"And as to how," Leif took over, "We used the same technique that Abbadon used on Kinver. We 'froze' them in a time portal until the being we were calling Abbadon was destroyed. Then I had Ruta set them free."

"Ruta? Is that who you were talking to when you were talking to the trees?"

"Well, I was asking the trees to let Ruta know what we were going to do. When they saw us come back, they told him where to find his village. By now he and Suzanne have returned to his village and set them free. We thought he would like some time with his family."

"Another reason you asked me to wait. You wanted to give them time to release the village, and Ruta to see his family?"

Sarah nodded, and I kept on walking, the implications of what they had said beginning to sink in.

I started to talk out loud. "So my mom knew I would need the bracelet to save the village she was going to visit? That probably means that we failed a few times. This time we succeeded."

As I talked to myself figuring things out, I started walking faster. When I saw Cahir loping out of the woods, I stopped walking and started running. People I loved were waiting for me, and I was finally ready to return to them.

Epilogue

Six months later…

Once again I stood on the hill overlooking my hometown of Eiddwen. This time was different. My mother Rowena and my father Darius were living there together. Both well. Both happy.

I had returned from the past to find everything as if Abbadon had never existed. Some people had no memory of him. Although those of us who had traveled in time remembered, and we would never forget. I knew it was supposed to be that way.

Before Sarah and Leif returned to their cabin, I had one last question for them. We were sitting around Aki's tea table with Niko when I asked the question that had been on my mind since seeing both the man Anne had fallen in love with, and the being that we had called Abbadon.

"The monster, the being that I saw, was one of the bored brothers wasn't it? My father's brother is the man Anne married. He was the real Abbadon, wasn't he?"

"Yes," Leif answered. "The brothers had returned to check on the dimensions and their experiment. One brother hated that nothing was happening in Erda. He was losing the bet that evil would take over Erda someday. He had bet that the real Abbadon would try to kill his brother, your father, and it was obvious that he had no intention of doing so.

"Not wanting to lose, the brother decided to speed things up. He stayed in Erda, and took over everyone, including Abbadon. He manipulated and controlled behind the scenes. However, when you defeated him with love, he lost the bet and his brother returned and took him away, leaving Anne free to marry your uncle, the real Abbadon."

"But this is another memory that only a few of you will have. Most of Erda only knows the real Abbadon and Darius. And Anne is still Queen of Abbadon's Kingdom as you are for your father's."

I hadn't been surprised to hear that answer. It made everything fall into place. It explained how Anne could fall in love with a monster. He wasn't one. And the trigger that began the destruction was the brother, not something that happened in Erda. In many ways it was a relief. Erda could continue in peace and harmony with nature and each other.

And even though some of us retained the memories of the destruction, we wouldn't let those memories keep us from celebrating our victory over evil. It would keep us alert to evil if it ever attempted to rise again.

In the restored Erda, the entire village of Dalry had never been touched, and no one other than a few of us had a memory of the thought-worms that had destroyed it.

Beru was back in her village of Kinver with her parents who had never left. Of the five men from Kinver that had helped us defeat Shatterskin and Deadsweep, only James and his daughter Liza remembered. Kit, who had died in the past, was still there. That sorrow had been lifted from my heart.

I continued to think of Kinver as a second home. They no

longer called me Hannah because I am happy to be Kara Beth. But they still call me daughter, and that is all I need.

I returned the star necklace to Liza. Seeing 4D is something I can call up at any time now. Like most of the magic I had forgotten, it all came back to me after Leif and I stopped the being that was calling himself Abbadon.

Instead of being afraid of my gifts and the responsibilities they carry, I am grateful. I know I won't abuse them. I have been tested, and I have passed that test. Not that I don't think there will be more, but my team, my friends, will be here if I need them.

Aki and Professor Link are now living together in the Castle, and Niko is enjoying not needing to hide his identity anymore. Both Aki and Niko carry the memory of their time in Abbadon's prison, but I'm not sure they realize it was Leif that had helped them escape.

I do know that Leif and Sarah still have many secrets that I don't know—yet. After all, Leif is a wizard and Sarah is an oracle. At least in Erda. Perhaps in the Earth Realm too.

Cahir stays in Eiddwen with his family most of the time. My father's housekeeper, Berta, is happy caring for my parents, who really don't need it anymore since my mother returned. But Berta and her skills keep their home and the village safe and happy. The only time the three of them left the village was when they traveled to the Castle for our wedding.

In royal terms, it had been a small wedding. Zeid and I didn't need anything other than our friends and family around us, and they all came. Even Teddy and the Ginete brothers had been there. Teddy cried huge tears the whole time, and couldn't stop whispering his favorite names for me as he watched the ceremony.

Even though my parents had stepped down from the throne

and had turned the Kingdom over to us, neither of us wanted to be anything other than Zeid and Kara Beth. The fact that we are now King and Queen hasn't changed us. It has only made us more grateful for what we learned and for the ones who supported us.

As we stood on the hill, remembering the past, the Priscillas got tired of waiting. They had made it halfway down the meadow before Zeid and I followed them, ready to continue our life together.

The danger had passed, but the thrill of traveling had not left me, and Zeid knew that, so I wasn't surprised when he asked, "Do you think you will want to do more traveling through portals, Kara Beth?"

As Lady streaked overhead heading to Eiddwen, I realized that answer was yes. But when, and where? That I didn't know. I had all the time in the world to find out.

Author's Note

As I wrap up this *Return To Erda* series I am thinking about where I want these characters to go, or are they happy where they are?

When I wrote *Karass*, the first book in the *Karass Chronicles*, I had no idea that it would turn into a series. If I had, I probably would have picked a different name. However, the series grew because readers and I liked the characters and wondered what happened to them.

Then when I wrote *Paragnosis*, the last book in the *Karass Chronicles*, I wondered what happened to some of the characters in the dimension they kept talking about. What was it like? Who lived there? And so I followed Hannah and a few of her friends from the Earth Realm to Erda.

Now another character from these two series has moved into the next one, *The Chronicles of Thamon*. Check out the series to see who it is.

If you have a character you would like to see more of, please let me know. Who knows, it could shape future books!

I have learned so much about writing these last few years. I hope to get better and better at the craft of writing as I write more stories. One thing that I have learned is how to follow the story and not try to force it.

That means there are many, many times—especially in *Abbadon*—where I was clueless as to what was going to happen next. Until I wrote it. Then I was as surprised as a reader would be. It was both terrifying and delightful. Or maybe it is as Suzanne says, beautifully terrifying.

If you would like to read a short prequel to these three series I'll send it to you for free.

It answers a few questions about the brothers who seeded Earth and Erda, and a little bit about where Suzanne really came from.

I'll tell you a secret: Earl and Ariel are not Suzanne's blood parents. And she has a sister Meg. More mystery. And another series, *The Chronicles of Thamon*.

Get this free short story here: becalewis.com/fantasy.

Love, Beca

PS
Be the first to know when there are new books, join my mailing list at becalewis.com/fantasy. Plus, I have some free giveaways. (Including that prequel to Karass and Erda and Thamon.)

Connect with me online:
Twitter: http://twitter.com/becalewis
Facebook: https://www.facebook.com/becalewiscreative
Pinterest: https://www.pinterest.com/theshift/
Instagram: http://instagram.com/becalewis
LinkedIn: https://linkedin.com/in/becalewis

OTHER BOOK SERIES BY BECA

The Karass Chronicles - Magical Realism

The Return To Erda Series - Fantasy

The Chronicles of Thamon - Fantasy

The Shift Series - Spiritual Self-Help

Perception Parables: - Fiction - very short stories

Advice: - Nonfiction
A Woman's ABC's of Life: Lessons in Love, Life and Career from Those Who Learned The Hard Way

ACKNOWLEDGMENTS

I could never write a book without the help of my friends and my book community. Thank you Jet Tucker, Jamie Lewis, Diana Cormier, and Barbara Budan for taking the time to do the final reader proof. You can't imagine how much I appreciate it.

A huge thank you to Laura Moliter for her fantastic book editing.

Thank you to the fabulous Molly Phipps at wegotyoucoveredbookdesign.com for the beautiful book covers for the *Erda* series.

Thank you to every other member of my Book Community who help me make so many decisions that help the book be the best book possible.

Thank you to all the people who tell me that they love to read these stories. Those random comments from friends and strangers are more valuable than gold.

And always, thank you to my beloved husband, Del, for being my daily sounding board, for putting up with all my questions, my constant need to want to make things better, and for being the love of my life, in more than just this one lifetime.

ABOUT BECA LEWIS

Beca writes books that she hopes will change people's perceptions of themselves and the world, and open possibilities to things and ideas that are waiting to be seen and experienced.

At sixteen, Beca founded her own dance studio. Later, she received a Master's Degree in Dance in Choreography from UCLA and founded the Harbinger Dance Theatre, a multimedia dance company, while continuing to run her dance school.

After graduating—to better support her three children—Beca switched to the sales field, where she worked as an employee and independent contractor to many industries, excelling in each while perfecting and teaching her Shift® system, and writing books.

She joined the financial industry in 1983 and became an Associate Vice President of Investments at a major stock brokerage firm, and was a licensed Certified Financial Planner for more than twenty years.

This diversity, along with a variety of life challenges, helped fuel the desire to share what she's learned by writing and talking with the hope that it will make a difference in other people's lives.

Beca grew up in State College, PA, with the dream of becoming a dancer and then a writer. She carried that dream forward as she fulfilled a childhood wish by moving to Southern

California in 1969. Beca told her family she would never move back to the cold.

After living there for thirty years, she met her husband Delbert Lee Piper, Sr., at a retreat in Virginia, and everything changed. They decided to find a place they could call their own which sent them off traveling around the United States. For a year or so they lived and worked in a few different places before returning to live in the cold once again near Del's family in a small town in Northeast Ohio, not too far from State College.

When not working and teaching together, they love to visit and play with their combined family of eight children and five grandchildren, read, study, do yoga or taiji, feed birds, work in their garden, and design things. Actually, designing things is what Beca loves to do. Del enjoys the end result.

Made in the USA
Las Vegas, NV
21 December 2020

14474090R00144